Dear Reader,

This book is labeled "A Classic Novel of Love" because it is indeed "a classic," originally published in 1983, and a "novel of love," shorter and narrower in scope than my more recent novels.

It was originally written under the Billie Douglass pseudonym. Since readers now know my real name, I am using that on this reissue. The only other change you will find is the cover design. The title is the original one, as is the story within.

I hope you enjoy reading FAST COURTING both as much as I enjoyed writing it, and as much as I enjoy rereading it today.

Barbara Delinsky

Recent Titles by Barbara Delinsky from Severn House

MOMENT TO MOMENT
SWEET EMBER
A TIME TO LOVE
VARIATION ON A THEME

FAST COURTING

Barbara Delinsky

This title first published in Great Britain 2003 by
SEVERN HOUSE PUBLISHERS LTD of
9–15 High Street, Sutton, Surrey SM1 1DF.
A paperback edition of this book was published in the
USA only in 1983 by Silhouette Books, a division of
Simon & Schuster, Inc., under the pseudonym of
Billie Douglass.
This first hardcover edition published in the USA 2003 by
SEVERN HOUSE PUBLISHERS INC of
595 Madison Avenue, New York, N.Y. 10022.

British Library Cataloguing in Publication Data

Delinsky, Barbara, 1945-
Fast courting
1. Women journalists - United States - Fiction
2. Love stories
I. Title
813.5'4 [F]

ISBN 0-7278-5996-X

Printed and bound in Great Britain by
MPG Books Ltd., Bodmin, Cornwall.

Fast Courting

one

AT THE INSTANT ANTONIA PHILLIPS WHIPPED into the office of *Eastern Edge* editor Bill Austen, she sensed something afoot. Of the magazine's working editorial staff, she was the last to arrive. Four faces turned her way, each bearing a trace of guilt. Instinct told her that the odd welcome had nothing to do with her tardiness.

"Ooooops . . ." she murmured, stopping just short of the threshold. "Why do I have the feeling my slip is showing?" It was purely a figure of speech, for, in fact, she wasn't wearing a slip. What she wore was a smart cropped-jacket wool suit of loden green, whose stylish split skirt required no assistance in falling softly to a point below her knee, where it met the rich leather of her boot. She was undeniably attractive, tall and slim, the image of confidence in her own casual way.

"Come on in, Nia," Bill gestured, smiling with a hint of mischief that made her all the more alert. "We were just talking about you."

"Mmmmmm." She raised a speculative brow. "I thought so." She settled into the only free chair and deposited her oversized shoulder bag on the floor, then fished a notebook and pen from it before sitting back. "I'm sorry I'm late. I spent longer with Humphrey at the theater than I'd intended. But the story's good." Her apology was to the entire group, though it was outwardly directed at Bill. Again, she sensed an odd air of anticipation. "Uh . . . is something wrong?" Her violet eyes widened in the silence. "You *did* get my message, didn't you?"

"We got it, Nia. And thanks for stopping to call." Bill's grin was overly indulgent, sufficiently out of character to add to her suspicions. He shrugged benignly. "We took the liberty of going ahead."

In a habitual gesture, she shook her head to flip the few windblown strands of her heavily layered mahogany hair into place. She needed no mirror to vouch for the acceptability of her appearance. Why, then, the continuing limelight?

"You were talking about *me?"* she repeated. Slowly, she perused the group, pertly challenging them to come forward with further information.

Priscilla Cole, the associate editor with whom she shared chores and an office, offered an indirect explanation. "We were discussing the feature assignments for the June issue."

That was no surprise. Hadn't it been the stated purpose of the meeting? This was March; they were right on schedule. "Great! Where were you before I so rudely interrupted?" Nia grinned, camouflaging curiosity in congeniality.

"The Ten Most Eligible Easterners." James Cabot, one of the two senior editors, supplied the clue, pronouncing each word carefully. He was middle-aged, intelligent and straightforward. Nia turned to stare at him.

"You've got to be kidding . . ." she chided.

Christopher Daly, the other senior editor, joined the exchange with a smug grin. "Nope."

Astonished, she looked at Priscilla. "You're *not* kidding."

The other woman simply shook her head.

"Bill?" Nia turned to their leader as a last resort.

"Why the surprise, Nia?" He was mildly critical. "We've discussed the possibility of doing this piece."

Nia winced. "To *discuss* it is one thing; to actually *plan* it, to put it on the schedule, is another. It's the kind of thing the scandal sheets do so well. We've always stayed a cut above." Her argument was not unfounded. *Eastern Edge* had established itself as a monthly magazine with class, appealing to a wide assortment of thinking people up and down the East Coast. It contained a balanced blend of humor, human interest, exposé and education and was both well written and beautifully presented. In the four years Nia had worked for the publication, she had never had cause for doubt.

"And we'll continue to stay a cut above, as you put it." Bill solemnly took command. "*Our* feature story will be done with taste and sophistication, and with just enough tongue-in-cheek humor to deflect any flack. We'll approach it with an attitude of intelligence rather than an eye for the spectacular.

It will be researched carefully and written by the best." He hesitated for a fraction of an instant to let his point sink in. "*You'll* be doing the men."

"*Me? The men?* Oh, no, you don't." Nia's gaze narrowed as she suddenly understood the nature of the apologetic looks cast her way by her colleagues. "I won't be saddled with it. Just because I wasn't here to defend myself—"

"It's got nothing to do with your lateness," Bill insisted, his customary curtness returning to his voice. "I'd decided to give you the assignment even before this meeting began."

"Why not . . ." She looked quickly around, but Priscilla was the only other female in the room. Priscilla Cole was a petite woman who was, at thirty-four, Nia's senior by five years. She was quiet and hardworking, excelling in articles that relied more closely on research and less directly on personal interviews. A talented writer, she was even more skilled as an editor, able to quickly diagnose and treat copy problems over which others might agonize for hours. But she was single and vulnerable, precisely the type who would be eaten alive by the nearest most-wanted man, Nia mused. Much as Nia was reluctant to handle this assignment, she couldn't, in good conscience, will it on Priscilla.

"Why not one of the staff writers?" she made a blind stab.

Bill only shook his head. "Not skilled enough. Or tested. In the hands of some of the staff writers, this piece could easily resemble something in those scandal sheets you scorn."

Nia's gaze shot to the men beside her. "Why not either James or Chris? They're competent enough." She grinned, only to have her amusement wiped away by Bill's summary dismissal.

"I want a woman to interview the men. After all, the piece should be written from a woman's point of view. You're the perfect choice." His expression held discouraging finality.

"The perfect choice?" she echoed in dismay. "I'm the *worst* choice, Bill. I hate eligible bachelors! You know that."

She swung around as Chris, who was sitting next to her, laughed. "Present company excluded, of course," he quipped, beaming endearingly.

"Of course." She recovered quickly, reaching over to squeeze his arm affectionately. She was genuinely fond of Chris, who had moved into the slot of senior editor soon after she'd joined *Eastern Edge* as a staff writer. He had remained a close friend when she convinced him that she wanted nothing more. Indeed, he had been one of the more vocal proponents of her appointment as associate editor the year before. Turning, she addressed Bill again. "*You* know what I mean."

"I know where you've *been,* Nia, if that's what you're getting at." His voice lowered with his head. "I think it's precisely that background that will make you much more critical in your analysis. Your piece will be that much more intelligent and less emotional."

As Nia shook her head, wisps of brown brushed her shoulders. "I don't know, Bill. I disagree with the whole thing on principle."

"What disturbs you?" James asked, succinct as always.

"I . . . I suppose it sounds too much like a one-way dating service. We *will* be including the phone numbers of these magnificent specimens, won't we?" she jibed facetiously.

James ignored her. "What if we concentrated, as I think Bill has in mind, on the real *character* of these people? What if we gave it a different slant? An in-depth slant? What if it were a documentary rather than an advertisement?"

His argument had some merit, yet she wasn't ready to admit it. "Aren't *you* uncomfortable with the idea of a feature on available men and women?" she shot back, drawling the last words in attempted humor. James was the most conservative of the lot; his outward support of the project surprised her.

"No." His smile was only slightly self-conscious. "I'll be doing the other half."

"The women?"

"I believe that's all that's left," he deadpanned. Had Nia not known James Cabot for such a long time, she might have found his wry wit unbalancing. But she was as fond of him as she was of Chris.

"You're a happily married man, James. Aren't you going to feel . . . uncomfortable . . . ?"

"Why would I? The job doesn't require that I proposition my subjects."

Priscilla spoke softly. "Don't you see, Nia? His marriage gives him an advantage of detachment, just as your . . . your . . ."

"Divorce." Nia supplied the blunt word when

her friend stumbled and blushed. These were the people she worked with every day of the week. They knew of the marriage that had caused her such distress and had finally disintegrated shortly before she'd come to work here. Boston had been David Phillips' hometown; as a celebrated sportswriter, he had left his mark here. It was ironic that he had relocated to Texas, whereas she had chosen to stay in the East. But she did love Boston. To date, the only drawback to her decision was the recognition factor of her name; the whole of New England seemed to know she'd been David's wife. Fortunately, the whole of New England *didn't* know the details of the marriage or subsequent divorce.

Priscilla's words cut into her thoughts. "You and James can approach this assignment from a more impartial viewpoint, since you're both, theoretically, immune."

"Now, just a minute!" Chris sat forward, ready to do gentle battle. "I wouldn't exactly call Nia 'immune' to men. I happen to know that she's no recluse."

Nia rolled her eyes heavenward in a plea for strength to face what was to come. "Ah, so this is let's-discuss-Nia's-social-life time?"

But Chris was insistent. "You *do* date. I've intercepted more than one of those deep-voiced phone calls from 'a friend.' Priscilla's trying to make you out to be some kind of . . . of . . . eunuch!"

"Eunuch? My God, that's priceless!" Nia burst into a spontaneous gale of laughter. "You see, I don't need any eligible bachelor to spice up my life when I've got you, Chris!" Forgetting her original objection to the assignment, she gave in to the ready relaxation that was part and parcel of these editorial gatherings. The give-and-take here was one of her favorite aspects of the job.

Bill saw his opportunity and seized on it. "What have you got against 'eligible bachelors,' Nia? I mean, after all, we're only asking you to write about them, not marry one."

Nia laughed again, enjoying herself with her friends despite the shadow of this unwelcome assignment. "I wouldn't do *that,* Bill, if you begged me on bended knee. I've had my fill of marriage, *and* of husbands who *see* themselves as eligible bachelors. In fact," she pressed her point, pleased that her thoughts were as rational, "I have serious doubts that I could consider any man as 'eligible' if he does himself."

Priscilla frowned. "I'm not sure I follow."

Nia turned to her patiently. "By simple virtue of the fact that a man considers himself to be one of the East's most eligible, he would be far too arrogant for me." She cocked her head in jest. "I prefer the modest man, the strong, silent type. And *he's* the one who would never consent to be interviewed."

"You're forgetting one thing." Bill exerted his authority once more. "The eligible easterners you'll be interviewing haven't chosen *themselves* for anything. *We've* chosen them."

"*Who* chose them?" Chris sallied with a smirk, then looked around the room. "I don't recall any democratic discussion."

"Democracy goes only so far," Bill rejoined. "It

was the senior echelon of management that chose the victims."

"Victims. Hmmph." Nia grimaced, then added under her breath, "They'll love every minute of the adulation."

"Say what you will," Bill went on undaunted, "but it's been decided. Unless, that is," his lips twitched at the corners, "any of you care to take on the publisher, the executive editor, the managing editor and myself."

As he had anticipated, there were no takers. Whereas the camaraderie among the present group was strong and lively, the holders of those other positions brought to the arena far greater formality and far less spontaneity. Bill Austen was, more often than not, a buffer between the groups.

Nia, for one, recognized the brick wall she faced. With a sigh of tentative resignation, she raised her eyes to Bill's. "Who *are* they, anyway . . . these unsuspecting souls?"

Bill cleared his throat, lifted a piece of paper from the haphazard pile on his desk and flipped a pair of bifocals to his nose. "The women first." As he proceeded to read, Nia listened carefully, jotting names down, noting that the list consisted of a college dean, an obstetrician, a state legislator, an interior designer and a marine biologist. Their names were vaguely familiar, though far from the very visible ones she had expected.

"What do you think, Nia?" Bill tested the editorial waters, following her reaction more closely than those of the others. She was evidently his main source of immediate worry.

"Not bad, Bill." She nodded, granting qualified approval. "They do seem to span the coast. Actually, I had expected a more . . . glamorous lot."

"Then perhaps you begin to see what we're aiming at. The undiscovered, so to speak."

Chris's eyes twinkled. "Virgin territory."

"Is that line of comment necessary?" Priscilla moaned.

James supported her. "She's right, Chris. It's irrelevant. As a matter of fact, I believe at least two of those ladies have been married before."

"Happens to the best of us . . ." Nia added her postscript instants before Bill quelled the banter.

"Ladies and gentlemen . . ." He rapped his pen on the desktop. "If you could control the color commentary until I complete this list, we might all be able to get back to work."

"That's right!" Chris seconded the suggestion. "Let's hear Nia's line-up. The suspense is killing me."

Nia leaned closer, delivered a stage-whispered "I love you, too," then began to write as Bill solemnly intoned the roster.

"The Honorable Jonathan Trent, Justice of the Supreme Court of Errors of the State of Connecticut; Thomas Reiss, native Vermont author; Paul Kiley, President and Chairman of the Board of the Landover Foundation; Arthur Wallis-Wright, Concertmaster of the Boston Symphony Orchestra; and, finally, Daniel Strahan, Head Coach of the New England Breakers."

The silence that prevailed as Nia stared at the names now glaring from her paper gave proof of her role as the outspoken one of the crew. It was as though the others were holding their breath, cautiously awaiting her reaction. Even Bill had to admit that her outbursts were usually well founded, though she was impulsive enough to speak up when it might be wiser to remain silently accepting. In many ways Bill found her a challenge. It was his job to temper her vehemence and help channel its underlying spirit into her writing. She was widely considered to be a superb journalist, but it was largely her ardor that made her work unique.

"Well . . . ?" he prodded at last. "How do they strike you?"

She continued to study the list, dark head downcast, violet eyes hidden from general view. To all appearances, she was immersed in thought. In reality, she grappled with a world of inner demons playing havoc with her past. Uncomfortable, she shifted in her chair. When she finally spoke, her voice was softer, more pensive.

"Interesting."

"Interesting." Bill nodded, mocking her passivity. "Is that all?"

"What more can I say?"

"Well, for openers, do you think you can write a good feature story around these five?"

She looked down at the list again, idly fingering the gold locket at her throat. "It's a varied group, just as the women are. They come from different areas. Different occupations. All of them relatively unfeatured—except Strahan. Why was he included?" Her attempts to keep her voice even were only marginally successful; even she heard its slight waver.

"What's wrong with Strahan?" Chris asked. "He's brilliant! The Breakers haven't done so well since the franchise was formed!"

It was Priscilla who stage-whispered, in a rare display of playfulness, "In case you hadn't heard, Chris is into basketball this year. Everybody loves a winner."

"Uh-uh." Chris held up his hand and eyed the two women in good-natured rebuke. "I've always been a basketball fan. It's just that *this* season I'm not afraid to admit it."

"Do you go to the games?" Nia asked.

"Occasionally. When I can get tickets. And, let me tell you, that's not so easy lately. It's been one sell-out crowd after the other."

"Do you follow the televised games?" There was method to Nia's questioning, but Chris hadn't caught on yet.

"You bet!" He fell right into her trap. "And that's how I know that Strahan is a wizard. He's put together a team that *works* like a team; he's the one who holds it together. His pregame interviews and postgame comments are amazing—precise, to the point, always accurate."

Nia smiled. "Thank you, Chris. You've made my point." She turned her sharpened gaze on Bill. "*That's* why I question Strahan's inclusion here. He's probably been interviewed ten times as often as the other four combined."

As though Bill had anticipated her argument, he nodded. "You're right about that. But what do you know about *him?* I mean the *person* Daniel Strahan. Forget basketball."

Nia's lips curved up mischievously. "Forget it? I don't know anything *about* it to forget! I've never been a fan of basketball!" If her declamation was a bit too intense, none of her colleagues noticed.

"That's good." Bill caught her eye and held it with a force that took his words a step further. "If you're divorced from the game you'll be able to put together an insightful, very different story about the man. You won't have to go near the court, if you choose not to."

The understanding between Nia and Bill was immediate and gratifying. He knew of her vulnerability, had glimpsed that flicker of pain that she usually covered so well. Of the group gathered here, only Bill seemed to realize that David Phillips had been a die-hard Breaker fan, that he had written up their games for years. Rarely had he missed a home game, or even one on the road. That was what he had especially loved—the road trips. While the players found them exhausting, David Phillips thrived on them. Nia knew she had no right to blame the Breakers for what had come between David and herself. But she couldn't deny the bad taste in her mouth that came with the mention of the New England Breakers.

"Anyway," Chris quipped, lounging back in his seat, "*I* can help you when it comes to the technical information." He held a hand out and studied his fingers. "I used to play myself. Unfortunately, there wasn't much of a need for a five-foot-four forward."

The laughter that filtered through the room lightened the air a bit. "And how tall is this Strahan?" Nia asked, curious as to what form of giant she would be facing.

James reeled off the statistics. "Six four. Short by present standards. When *he* played—that was roughly ten years ago—they didn't come so tall. In his heyday, he weighed in at 190. From the looks of him today, he hasn't gained a pound."

Bill patted his rounding belly. "That's nice," he murmured, half to himself. "Exercise. That's the key. But what can *I* do? I'm stuck behind a desk all day."

"You could always run with me during the lunch hour," Chris offered. "Less time to eat."

"Why not have Gail pack you a salad?" Priscilla grinned. "You know, a little cottage cheese, a few fruit slices, some melba toast . . ."

Nia joined the attack, welcoming the respite. "I think he gets *too* much exercise," she spoke.

"*Too* much?" James challenged.

"Too much *arm* exercise," she specified with a grin.

Chris eyed her askance. "What are you talking about?"

"You know." She smiled broadly as she moved her hand in a repeated lap-to-mouth motion. "Too much arm exercise. After all, it takes some effort to shovel it in." She turned mirthfully to Bill. "What do you think, Bill?" She mimed his own recent request.

"I think," Bill cleared his throat and frowned, "that we've gotten off the track. If there's no further discussion right now on the eligible easterners feature, we'll move on—"

"Hold it!" Nia exclaimed. "*I* still have discussion on that piece. Is there *no one else* who can do it?" Bill shook his head emphatically, feeling little remorse in the wake of the stinging, if humorous, assault on his waistline. Her eyes crinkled at the corners. "You're sure?"

"Absolutely. What's the matter, Nia? You're *really* not up to it?"

"Oh, I can *do* it," she replied, using the inflection of her voice to make the point. "It's more a question of whether I can do it *well,* considering the prejudice I feel before I've even begun."

"You'll do it well," Bill informed her, glancing over the rim of his glasses, then taking them off and tossing them onto the desk. "I'll see to that!"

His words returned to haunt her later that day as she sat in her office pondering the assignment. Bill had "seen to it" in the past, particularly at the start of her career, when he'd guided her through several tough assignments. That she had the writing skill was never at issue. What disturbed her most was effecting the most comfortable balance between intellect and emotion so that her writing remained a feature story rather than a personal editorial.

Her first big assignment had been to write a feature on the Plymouth II Nuclear Power Plant, presenting the controversy as it had unfolded. The personalities involved, both for and against, had been explosive. Nia had her own very firm opinion on the subject, and it had been a constant struggle to hold that opinion in check. Bill had helped then, pointing out phrasing that betrayed her inner emotion so subtly that even she hadn't been aware of it. With minor wording changes and a closer rein held on the whole, the final feature became a source of pride to her.

That had been three and a half years ago. Since then, there had been features on such vital and varied topics as police work, venture capitalism and genetic research. On each issue she had started from scratch, reading, researching, learning from the ground floor up. By nature, she had taken positions as her writing progressed. It was Bill who helped minimize the overspill, forming an end product that was thoroughly professional and liberal in its allowance for differing opinions. Such was the reputation of *Eastern Edge* as a publication; of that, too, Nia was proud.

Now, she sifted through the papers on her desk, gathering the rough draft of the story she'd written that afternoon. It was an analysis of live theater in Boston, its history and promise, as well as its reality. Many hours' work had been spent reading up on the history of the various theaters that had, over the years, been the pre-Broadway drill grounds. Additional hours had gone into interviews with the people involved, both in the past and the present. Just this morning she had spent two hours with Samuel Humphrey, the owner of the new, startlingly elaborate theater-opera house-philharmonic hall complex downtown. It was this interview that had made her late for the editorial meeting.

A frown creased her brow as her gaze drifted idly around the office. It was a comfortable-sized room, bright and well-kept, modern, as was the entire building, one of the more recent additions to Boston's clustered skyline. No, she couldn't find fault with Bruce McHale, the magazine's owner, on *that* score. He believed that his people worked best in pleasant surroundings. Hence, this office.

The walls and desks were white, the carpeting and obligatory bulletin boards burgundy. All else was done in crisp navy blue, from padded desk chairs to lamp shades to ashtrays and file cabinets. Wood was markedly absent. Rather, the furnishings and accessories were of the highest quality vinyl, formica, steel or fabric—all blended to preclude harshness while allowing for clear lines of utility. The room held two desks, each in its own work area, delineated by a freestanding, open bookshelf. It was through the fronds of a spindly asparagus fern on one of these shelves that Nia's eyes met Priscilla's.

"Something wrong, Nia? You've been daydreaming longer than usual."

Nia's gaze moved about the room once more. "I was just reminding myself how lucky we are that McHale believes in the finer things in life. We could be set up in an ancient flea-trap."

Priscilla chuckled. "There aren't many of those left now. Urban renewal has done wonders. Believe it or not, this very area used to be one of the seediest parts of town. You would never have dared pass through here alone, and if you happened to *work* here, chances are you were a . . . a . . ."

"I get the drift," Nia indulgently rescued her friend. "But you native Bostonians take your age for granted. I grew up on the West Coast where, historically, at least, things are younger. There is a remarkable beauty in some of the landmarks here—the Custom House, the Old City Hall, Paul Revere's house. Then, once you get out to Lexington and Concord, another whole world opens up."

"You do like it here, don't you?"

"Yes. I'm glad I stayed." Her implication was clear and triggered a new train of thought.

"Say," Priscilla burst out, "have you heard anything about the *Western Edge* assignment? Wasn't Bill going to let you know this week?"

Nia thrust her fingers through her thick mane of mahogany layers and sighed. "No word yet. But there's no rush; my family isn't going anywhere. I'd like to see them, and it would be super to combine a visit with work." She grinned conspiratorially. "One of the advantages of working for a magazine that has a sister publication on the opposite coast!"

"Further kudos for Bruce McHale," Priscilla joked, lifting an imaginary goblet in toast. "For interior decorating *and* a generous travel allowance."

"Hmmm." Nia glanced at the calendar on the bulletin board by her desk. "I do seem to have plenty of travel coming up, what with research to be done on the Amish in Pennsylvania and the low-down on life on Washington's Ambassador's Row. Those are all immediate; then there's that assignment Bill gave me this morning. . . ."

That was the true source of the nagging doubts in the back of her mind. For some reason, this particular assignment had struck her the wrong way.

"It's still bothering you, isn't it?" Priscilla homed in on the problem.

"I suppose so. I wish he could have found someone else."

"But, why, Nia? He was right. You're perfect for this feature. If anyone can handle men, you can." There were both admiration and a hint of envy in Priscilla's voice, but Nia was too immersed in her own dilemma to appreciate that.

"That's just it! I don't *want* to have to handle anyone. I picture these five men as enamored of their own 'availability.' If they've agreed to the feature, they're bound to be cocky, to say the least."

"But . . . they haven't. Have they?"

Nia frowned. "Haven't what?"

"Agreed. I got the impression that *you'll* be making the initial contacts."

"Oh, Lord," Nia groaned. "I'd assumed that someone got their OK."

"Someone *will*. You." At her friend's distress, Priscilla offered encouragement. "Look, Nia, you'll do a great job. You write beautifully and you're much more sophisticated and socially poised than so many others. Besides, you've taken on other assignments where you've had doubts."

"Doubts?" Nia's eyes widened to bright violet saucers. "This verges on sheer embarrassment! What am I supposed to do—call each of these men and say 'Congratulations! You've been chosen . . .' and so on?"

"Well, if they're as egotistical a bunch as you'd like to believe, they'll eat up anything you serve to them. You may feel embarrassed now, but I can assure you, based on what you've done in the past, that the finished product will be outstanding."

Nia smiled warmly. "Thanks. You're good for *my* ego, Priscilla. I'm going to need your bolstering through *this* one!"

"Listen, if it's bothering you, why don't you get to work on it early? I mean, I know that you've got two months to write the story, but if you think that it may hang over your head, why not get it over with?"

Nia took a deep breath, held it, then exhaled. "You may be right about that. I suppose that once I get into it, it won't be so bad."

"That's the spirit!" Her friend beamed, then sobered quickly as Nia shot her a pointed look.

"Don't get too enthused, Priscilla, or I may just let *you* take over for me. Bill would never know the difference."

But the other woman knew the threat was an empty one. "Oh, he'd know! I haven't quite got your flair. That's all there is to it." This time, mixed in with admiration was a touch of relief, and that Nia *could* appreciate. When she would have ribbed her friend about it, her telephone beeped. Even its gentle sound had been prescribed by Bruce McHale as an antidote to the stereotypical chaos of the publishing world.

As it happened, it was the art department seeking information for sketches to accompany an article on the revival of the process of old-fashioned quilting. Nia hadn't written the article herself; rather, she'd edited the work of one of the newer staff writers. With the copy set now, it was simply a matter of deciding on the "accessorizing."

Of her own choice, Nia had researched the history behind each of the five patterns chosen for illustration; she'd found it to be fascinating. Even now, as she talked with the art director, she was easily engrossed. One day, she'd vowed, she would write a book on the arts and crafts of colonial America and their tie-in with the colonial personality. But *that* was for another time, a time when she had greater leisure and less need to exhaust herself in the day-to-day world of work. Now, the busy pace suited her, as did the unending variety of her job. All told, she spent less time brooding about David Phillips and the life they might have had than she would have done at a job with more regular hours. The excitement of *Eastern Edge* was right up her alley—despite occasional set-backs such as she'd had that morning.

It was that very set-back which she pondered when, the matter settled and the conversation ended, she hung up the phone. Priscilla had gone back to her own work, leaving a legacy of advice. Nia considered that advice as she rocked back in her chair with an eye on the calendar. Perhaps Priscilla was right. Perhaps it *was* better to get it over with. In those childhood days of clean-your-plate-now, Nia, hadn't she always eaten the liver first?

Pen in one hand, phone book in the other, she lifted the receiver. If nothing more, she would make the initial overtures to each of her targeted subjects. A short introductory interview might be helpful in giving her direction, in letting her know with what she was dealing. To date, this was her most distasteful assignment. Gritting her teeth, she got to it.

One week later, her teeth were still gritted. Of the five "most eligible easterners" on her list, four had been reached and had graciously, if somewhat reluctantly, agreed to an initial meeting. Those four were Trent, Reiss, Kiley and Wallis-Wright. She had been surprised at their graciousness, quite frankly startled at their reluctance. It seemed that her preconceptions might have been overjudgmental; each man seemed as wary of her as she was of him. No, the cause of her clenched jaw had little to do with the four she'd contacted. It was the fifth who rankled her.

Strahan. Daniel Strahan. "Eligible," yet elusive. "Available," yet nowhere to be found. Christopher Daly had assured her that the Breakers were home for two weeks of near-nightly games, with the heat of the season in sight. Yet none of her calls were returned, not the slightest acknowledgment made of her efforts to reach the head coach. She had even gone so far as to switch on the television the night before—to assure herself that there was, indeed, a man named Strahan at the Breakers' helm. Sure enough, standing absorbed at the sidelines, so the commentator said, was the coach. From the camera's distant perspective he was an indistinct figure in a shirt and tie, casual blazer, darker-shaded slacks, with a headful of thick, dark hair. That was Strahan, all right; she was up enough on faces in the news to recognize him quickly. In the next instant, she had flipped the switch and darkened the screen. Basketball was *not* her thing!

Reaching for the phone, she frowned in response to those memories she'd rather not face. Her finger punched at the buttons of the number she now knew by heart. The switchboard operator's sing-song "Weston Arena . . . May I help you?" could as easily have been a recording and a broken one at that, for the number of times she'd heard it.

"Daniel Strahan, please." She spoke evenly, curbing her annoyance for the sake of civility, drumming her fingernails on the laminated desk surface in frustration.

"One moment, please." Click. Hold. Hold. Hold. "I'm sorry. Mr. Strahan doesn't seem to be in his office. Would you care to leave a message?"

Sighing at the expected, Nia responded, "This is Antonia Phillips from *Eastern Edge.* I've been trying to reach Mr. Strahan for the better part of a week. My messages have never been returned. He *does* pick them up, doesn't he?"

"Oh, yes, miss."

"Is he *in* the building?"

"I couldn't tell you that for sure." Couldn't? Or wouldn't? The end result was the same.

"Do you know of any time that I *might* reach him there?"

"Hold, please." Click. Hold. Hold. Hold. At last the faceless voice returned. "A practice is scheduled here tomorrow morning from ten to twelve-thirty. You might be able to catch him at either end."

Progress. At least Nia now knew he'd be in the building then. "Thank you. I *will* try tomorrow. Oh . . . perhaps you could leave a message that I called again. That's Phillips, P-H-I—"

"I have it, Ms. Phillips." For the first time, there was a hint of humanity in the sound. "Unless, that is, it's changed since yesterday . . . ?" And humor.

Nia couldn't suppress a small smile. It wasn't this woman's fault that Daniel Strahan lacked the common courtesy to return her calls. "No, it's the same. Thank you." It was only after she hung up that she looked at her calendar. Kiley. Landover Building, Worcester. Ten.

So it was that, at eleven-thirty the next morning, she found herself on the Mass Turnpike headed east, back from Worcester to Boston. Weston was roughly forty-five minutes away en route; the turnpike exit was no more than three minutes from the arena itself.

Her mind wandering, Nia recalled the hullabaloo surrounding the stadium's construction ten years before. She had been a sophomore at Radcliffe then and had just met David. He, for one, was ebullient in anticipation of a new sports showcase. Others were not as enthused. The local residents feared the regular and repeated invasion of an unruly army of sports fans. The sports fans themselves temporarily resisted their peremptory ousting from downtown Boston. The entrepreneurial interests spoke of free access, easy parking, increased capacity, greater profits . . . and won.

She and David were a regular twosome by the time ground had been broken in March of that year. By May, when they broached the topic of marriage to her parents, construction was underway. By June, the site was a mad array of steel and concrete in action, while Nia carried on weekly long-distance arguments with her parents in attempts to convince them that she loved David, that their fifteen-year age difference was inconsequential, that her marriage would not disrupt her education. By July, when they eloped, the outline of the arena had begun to take shape. There were the inevitable delays, the complications and hints of cost overruns that plagued the project; through it all, their fledgling marriage reflected similar growing pains. It wasn't, however, until October of the following year, well after Nia and David celebrated their first wedding anniversary, that he covered the gala opening and the maiden game played by the Breakers in this, their new home.

A tractor-trailer passed on the right, then veered into the middle lane directly in front of Nia, tearing her thoughts from past to present as she hit her horn. Slowing to let the truck move away, she was grateful for the distance and the return of wide open space on all sides, and let her thoughts drift to her current assignment.

Paul Kiley had been a pleasant surprise. He had seen her right on time, had been polite and relaxed once she had explained her objectives, which she, in turn, was able to do with an astounding degree of conviction considering her original reluctance. What she had planned as a thirty-minute introductory interview had swelled into an hour and a half. Kiley had given her the time, excusing himself only to take the occasional phone call that came through. The interview had flowed; both of them had sensed its smoothness and run with it. For Nia's part, she had, indeed, begun to get a feel for the man and his lifestyle. He'd given her food for thought, plenty to research before she met him a second, and most likely final, time. It hadn't been half as bad as she had expected.

Weston. The sign was suddenly before her as though out of the blue, evoking a purely reflexive tremor from within. It was nearly twelve-ten. If the switchboard operator was correct, Strahan would be occupied by team practice for another twenty minutes. If she was lucky enough to avoid any traffic, she might just make it into Boston and to her telephone in time to catch him before he left the arena. But if she missed him again . . . and if he continued to slam-dunk her messages into his wastebasket . . .

With a flick of her head to shake her hair back from her forehead, she took the Weston exit, paid her toll, and headed for the arena. She was so close; it was too good an opportunity to miss. After all, she would have to come out here to interview him *some* day.

In defense against bitter memories, Nia concentrated on what she knew about Daniel Strahan. It was, in fact, very little. He had been a Breaker great, a star in his playing days. During the four years that he'd been head coach of the team, its record had steadily improved. This year the Breakers were headed for the playoffs. It was impossible to live in Boston and *not* know that, even allowing for her distaste of the sport. The daily papers were filled with the jubilant word, which ranked up there with politics, foreign affairs and the economy on the front page.

The parking lot was mammoth. Nia pulled into a free space near the arena, shifted and turned off the ignition, then sat. Surely there was something else she knew about Daniel Strahan, some little tidbit deep back in her memory bank. Nothing. But why? With the gaggle of dirt-hungry reporters who covered each game and conducted those infamous pregame and postgame interviews, certainly the man's life was an open book. Why did she know nothing?

As she stepped from her car and locked the door she had second thoughts about this drop-in visit. Usually she was better prepared; even in Kiley's case, she had studied a preliminary bio. Granted, she hadn't planned on confronting Daniel Strahan today. Perhaps he'd even manage to evade her now.

Her violet gaze, wide and uneasy, took in the imposing arc of the arena's structure, sending a chill through her. *This* was why she knew nothing about Daniel Strahan; everything about basketball in general, and this place in particular, made her uncomfortable. Had it not been for Bill Austen and his supposedly brilliant idea she wouldn't be here now. For that matter, had Daniel Strahan the social grace to return even one of her calls, she would not have felt at such a distinct disadvantage. What if he actually *refused* to see her? That would be downright unpleasant. On the other hand, she smiled at the clever thought, such a reception could be just enough to convince Bill to find another "eligible easterner," freeing her from the world of basketball once more.

Bolstered by this vague hope, Nia entered the Arena and looked around. Despite the hundreds and hundreds of hours her ex-husband had spent in the building, this was her very first visit. Though she had picked up David many a time outside, she had never ventured within. Strangely, she felt as if she were at the scene of a crime. It seemed perfectly in keeping when a uniformed security guard stopped her.

"Looking for someone?" he asked blandly.

"Uh, yes. I'm here to see Daniel Strahan." She spoke with the confidence of her professional position.

"He's busy."

"I know. There's a practice that should be over soon. I'm early." In some situations Nia would have instantly identified herself as being with the magazine. Here, intuition held her back. Security guards were often more like bodyguards; if this one had an aversion to press people, he'd never allow her entrance.

"Does he know you're here?" the guard asked, his gaze narrowed in suspicion.

Nia bluffed. "I've left him several messages."

"You a friend?"

Unwilling to lie, she offered a simultaneous smile and a shrug, letting her slightly provocative head-tilt suggest what it would. It did.

"Ah. Girlfriend. About time." To her astonishment, he seemed utterly satisfied. Turning, he pointed toward a ramp. "Go on over there, make a left through those doors and up the steps. You can watch."

Watch basketball practice? There was little she wouldn't rather do. She nearly blurted out as much on impulse. Then it occurred to her that to argue might mean antagonizing the guard. It would be wiser to suffer through the last of the practice, then ask directions to Strahan's office.

With a polite nod and a smile of appreciation, she did as the guard had suggested, soon finding herself low in the stands opposite the side of the floor where the team seemed centered. Sliding as unobtrusively as possible into the nearest seat, she opened her notebook, determined to ignore the ongoing practice in protest against the game and what it had done to her life.

To her chagrin, her powers of concentration left much to be desired. Much as she might glue her eyes to the notes she'd made that morning in Worcester, her ears picked up every nuance of the action on the court. There was the call of instructing voices—was that *his* voice?—as plays were called, and the slap and squeal of sneaker treads against the floor as each play was executed. There was the murmur of conversation between teammates, oaths of fatigue, gasps of exertion. There was the occasional smack of flesh on flesh as two players accidentally collided with one another and, of course, the resounding thud of the ball as it hit the floor. Ironically, as if it was irrelevant, the victorious swish of a basket was drowned out by the sounds of the players proceeding to the next drill.

Her eyes drifted up against her will to scan the play for a moment before moving on to the reason for her presence, the focal point of the practice as well, the coach. To her surprise, he wore a Breaker warm-up suit, as did those players who were sidelined for one reason or another. She had always assumed that coaches were more formally dressed, symbolically removed from the team.

Daniel Strahan was well in control. From where she sat, his deep-toned commands slowly set themselves apart from the other sounds by an air of subtle authority. Intrigued, she looked more closely.

There were perhaps nine players on the court, alternately running through plays and gathering around the coach. Several other players followed the action, as did three other men beside Strahan. Assistant coaches? Trainers? The words popped into her mind, gleaned from long-ago discussions she'd overheard between David and his fellow addicts. As to the specific role of an assistant coach or a trainer, she was ignorant. Indeed, even the daily duties of the head coach remained a mystery.

Inevitably her gaze returned to Strahan. Standing alone for the moment, calling commands with one hand on his hip and the other pointing from one player to another, he was tall and lean, broad of shoulder and narrow of hip. His hair was dark, very dark, and casually mussed. As she watched he took the basketball to demonstrate a particular evasive move; the action was lithe and fluid, exhibiting the superb coordination which had, in part, been responsible for his own success as a player. Back on the sideline, he stood briefly at the center of the group. To her surprise and marginal amusement, he was the shortest one there.

But surprise and amusement turned to caution as she saw the guard who had directed her approach Strahan. The players returned to the court; the two men stood head to head. After a few moments Strahan looked up toward Nia.

For a few seconds she was aware only of how out of place she must look, dressed conservatively yet with a definite feminine flair in a lace-edged sweater, full skirt and high-heeled pumps. Nia had anticipated spending the morning in corporate circles, the afternoon in the office. More casual clothes might have been appropriate here . . . but, then, she hadn't planned on stopping until the arena's proximity to her route had tempted her. Now she wished she'd resisted that temptation. Strahan was scowling; that was clear despite the distance.

Fighting the urge to sink lower in her seat, Nia held his gaze stubbornly, reminding herself of the deskful of messages he had seen fit to ignore. The guard turned and walked away. For a moment longer Strahan stared. Then something on the floor caught his eye and his attention, and Nia was left in peace.

Peace. What a strange word, she mused, as she slowly recovered from the powerful, if short, visual interchange. She had known peace when David was on the road, leaving her to the writing she thought would establish her as a respected professional entity. But the rumors of infidelity had crept up on that peace, shattering it completely in that final, cruel year.

Breathing deeply, she forced her attention back to the court, where her eyes had blindly continued to follow the practice. Now it was over. The shortest of the men with Strahan—yes, she decided arbitrarily, the trainer—handed out towels to each passing player. In a slow procession they headed for the tunnel to the locker room and were swallowed up, one by one, in the darkened cavity. A few stragglers remained, one of them Strahan. Her pulse jerked when he looked up at her once more. He stood confidently, both hands cocked on his hips, as though he were awaiting something.

"You can come with me now."

Nia's head spun around to find the same guard in the aisle. "Oh, you startled me!" she exclaimed, gathering her wits, wondering whether she was being taken into custody or expelled. Neither turned out to be the case. For, moments later, after a seemingly endless trek through aisles and up corridors, she was ushered into Daniel Strahan's office.

"He'll be right with you," was the curt message as the guard turned and left. Nia watched his exit, feigning self-confidence, but feeling maddeningly unsure.

When the hall beyond the door was empty once more, she turned to peruse her cell. The office was actually quite large, but made immeasurably smaller by the wall-to-wall collection of basketball memorabilia. There were pennants and pictures, statuettes and full-sized trophies. There were certificates and citations and plaques. All told, there must have been half a dozen basketballs at random spots, several on stands marked for one historic game or another. There were papers, books and a stack of precariously piled movie reels. There was not one item she would call truly personal—no family photographs, no hint of the man independent of the game. It was basketball, all of it. Nia shuddered in aversion.

Frustrated and impatient, she threw herself into the chair on the opposite side of the desk. Where was he? She looked at her watch, then looked again five minutes later. It was bad enough that he'd never returned her calls, but to purposely keep her waiting was even worse. Was this the way he customarily treated women? No wonder he was still "eligible"!

When her waiting reached the ten-minute mark, she shifted in her seat. Desperately, she tried to blot out the room's pervading decor, but distaste welled up in her stubbornly. It was a game, big boys, little boys—what difference? This one had obviously never learned manners! Fifteen minutes had passed and she began to seethe; another five found her livid. Hadn't she paid her dues as a basketball widow long ago? Damn it! There were other things to do in life besides wait in a congested office, competing for air space with an overblown collection of inane souvenirs!

Pushing herself from the chair, she hoisted her bag to her shoulder, threw her wool reefer over the crook of her elbow and stormed to the door. There she came to an abrupt halt. For, standing at his full height, no longer overshadowed by the distracting presence of giants, was Daniel Strahan. And if *she* was angry, he was no less so.

two

HIS EYES WERE DARK AND PIERCING. HIS voice shot sharply through her. "Leaving already?" he asked tautly.

"Already?" she heard herself echo, stunned for but a brief instant before rage took over. "*Already?* I've been waiting here for twenty minutes now." That twenty-minute stretch combined with the anger of the past to explode in a reaction that would not be tempered. "Is this your idea of good public relations? If so, you've been sadly misguided." Her eyes flashed. "You could have sent someone in to say you'd been delayed, or even called yourself from that precious locker room of yours. But, then, you're allergic to telephones, aren't you? That must be why you never returned my calls." It was only when she paused to catch her breath that Nia realized the extent of her outburst. Every muscle in her body was tensed.

Daniel Strahan didn't flinch. He was neither intimidated nor phased. Rather, he stared down from his superior height, wearing a mask of dark indignance. "I didn't ask you here."

"Your . . . henchman *escorted* me here—"

"After you had very conveniently announced yourself to him as my girlfriend."

Nia tipped her chin up in defiance. "I never did that."

The coach's gaze narrowed dangerously. "Then why did he report it?"

"He chose to draw that conclusion."

"And who *are* you?"

"My name is Antonia Phillips. I've been trying to reach you on the phone all week."

"So you've opted for a different method?"

Now that she had revealed her name, Nia felt a heightened sense of responsibility for her behavior. She owed it both to the magazine she represented and to herself to look and act the part of the professional. "As it happened," she succeeded in lowering her voice, "I had an appointment earlier this morning in Worcester. The arena was right on my way back to Boston. Since I'd been unable to reach you by phone, I thought I'd take a stab and stop here."

Daniel Strahan's initial vexation seemed slightly eased by her explanation. Relieved, Nia took the time to notice that he was newly showered and dressed in a blazer and slacks. His hair was black and damp, his jaw clean shaven. Aside from the harshness lingering in his gaze, he could actually be classed as attractive.

For an instant, doubt mingled with that harshness. "Antonia Phillips?" He sought to make the identity.

"Anto*ni*a," she corrected automatically. Her name had been mispronounced for the better part of her life; it was a matter of the emphasis on the wrong syllable.

"Anto*ni*a," he repeated it properly. She thought she saw a quirk at the corner of his lips, but it vanished before she could either verify its presence or contemplate its intent. "Antonia Phillips." His brows drew together. *"Eastern Edge?"* At her nod he drew himself up even taller, if that was possible. "Ah," he exhaled slowly. "*Those* messages."

Nia couldn't contain her barb. "Does that mean that you're inundated with daily messages from many sources?"

"The press is persistent."

"We're not exactly 'the press,' " she inserted firmly.

Again she caught a trace of that quirk that did nothing more than appear, then disappear, leaving her distinctly off-balance. "Oh?" he asked. "I suppose it's a matter of semantics. *Eastern Edge* may be a magazine—and a fine one at that—but," he spoke evenly, as though treading more cautiously in direct consideration of his claim, "it still qualifies as the media." To further disconcert her, he took a step into the room, closed the door behind him and leaned against it.

Nia feld oddly trapped and strangely awkward. He was tall and commanding, as imposing a figure as she had ever seen. She was the intruder here, totally out of her element. Indeed, Daniel Strahan now studied her as though *she* were the oddity, rather than his sizable comrades.

When he spoke again he was fully in charge. "No further argument?"

"Not on that," she answered truthfully. "It's not that terribly important."

"Then what *is* important enough to merit your daily calls and finally bring you here today?"

"I'd like to speak with you."

"That's obvious."

Nia knew that she had to do something to break the verbal deadlock, for her own composure's sake if not for purposes of her mission. For a woman who usually controlled an interview, she felt sadly deficient. "Uh," she looked around, then gestured toward the chair she'd left in such fury earlier, "would you mind if I sat down?" Where *had* that fury gone? It seemed to have been supplanted by an unexpected perplexity. For the first time she asked herself who Daniel Strahan really was. Without doubt, her curiosity was piqued.

The object of her musings nodded his permission, waited for her to sit, then walked around his desk and slowly slid into his own chair. His eyes barely left hers. "Now, what can I do for you, Miss Phillips?"

"It's *Mrs.* Phillips," she corrected, not knowing why she had added that when it was truly irrelevant. "But I'd rather you called me Antonia."

"Mrs.?" His gaze flicked to her bare left hand in obvious challenge.

"I'm divorced."

He nodded, lifting steepled fingers to his chin in a pensive pose accentuated by the dark, dark brown of his eyes. At that moment he reminded Nia more of a thinker, a man of letters, than an athlete. She wondered what he did in his spare time. Then she chided herself; she, of all people, knew that there was precious little spare time in the world of professional sports. Aside from the off-season, which was often filled with camps, appearances, practices and the like, the professional athlete lived a life on the run. Hadn't David's life with the Breakers been much like that? There had been basketball, basketball and more basketball. Then, when that was over, there was always basketball.

"David Phillips." As though he had reached a profound conclusion, Daniel's deep voice bluntly offered up the very name that had been in Nia's mind seconds earlier.

She stiffened. "Excuse me?"

"David Phillips. Were you his wife?"

"David Phillips?"

"He covered the team during most of my playing years. I vaguely recall hearing something about a wife . . ." He frowned, confused, then shook his head. "Forget I said that. It couldn't have been you."

Overcoming her initial shock at his mention of David, Nia yielded to curiosity. "Why not?"

Daniel spoke more softly, but without hesitation. "For one thing, he was much older than you are. For another, he was too much of a ladies' man to be married to someone with your good looks. If he'd been married to you, he never would have wandered."

The compliment did nothing to take the edge off the bluntness of Daniel's assessment. Nia had learned the hard way about David; even now, so long after the divorce, the sting of his infidelity seared her. Whether it was the haunted cast of her eyes or the sudden pallor of her skin that gave her away, she was never to know. But Daniel instantly sensed his *faux pas.*

"I'm sorry. I shouldn't have said that," he offered in a surprisingly gentle tone. "He *was* your husband?"

"He was," she whispered.

"I *am* sorry, Antonia."

"For what?" She mustered her poise and produced a hollow laugh. "For my being married to David or for your having pegged him so accurately in front of me?"

"Both." He took a deep breath, hesitated, then slowly smiled. "Did I pronounce the name right this time?"

More than anything that had come before, Daniel Strahan's smile took her breath away. It was like a magic door, inching open to reveal a wealth of warmth beyond. There was an honesty about it, as well as equal shares of strength and vulnerability. Above all it was human—a far cry from the superstar image she had been prepared to meet.

Momentarily tongue-tied, she struggled to recall what he was talking about. "Uh, yes, you said it right. Actually, my friends call me Nia. It simplifies things."

"Antonia is beautiful." His eyes were as intense as they'd been before, but with a wholly different sheen. "It fits you."

Against her will, a pink flush crept to her cheeks, adding innocent pleasure to her face. Just as his praise brought a return of her color, it bolstered the ego that was always rebruised at mention of David. Either Daniel Strahan was an expert at handling the press or, contrary to her original assertion, he was a whiz with women. It occurred to her that he had read her perfectly, understanding in those brief instants what she must have suffered. Once more she wondered about *his* private affairs and the course of events that had led to his being "eligible." Which reminded her of her purpose. This was as good a time as any to broach it, while his defenses were down.

Self-conscious beneath his continued stare, she cleared her throat. "Mr. Strahan, as I said, I'm with *Eastern Edge.*" At her mention of the magazine the shutters closed, rendering him the carefully controlled head coach once more. "The reason I've tried to reach you . . . the reason I stopped by today . . . is that we're running a feature in the June issue for which we'd like to interview you."

His voice was kind but firm. "I don't give interviews."

"Of course you do!" she argued, her spirit miraculously and fully reinstated. "You give televised interviews before and after every game, not to mention your talks with the sportswriters."

His gaze was level. "That's what I'm paid to do."

"How does that differ from *my* request?"

"*You* tell *me,*" he commanded. "Is it basketball you're writing about?"

Earlier he had seemed to trap her physically. Now the snare was intellectual. "No."

"Then . . . what?"

"You."

His smile this time was a ghost of the other, a mere formality. "So, we've come full circle. I repeat: I don't give interviews."

Nia had no intention of accepting defeat so easily. While she had originally fought with Bill against the feature, here she would champion it for all she was worth. "Any special reason?"

"Many."

"How about one," she coaxed him softly.

Dropping his hands to his lap, Daniel leaned back in his chair, as though protectively immersing himself in the surrounding memorabilia. "My private life is my own. It has no place here."

"You don't think that your fans would like to hear about it?"

He inclined his head. "I'm sure they would." His terseness bore a finality Nia was committed to resist.

"You don't enjoy pleasing them?"

"On the contrary. I *do* enjoy pleasing them. *On the court.* That's what they pay for when they buy a ticket. That's what the ownership pays for when I sign a contract. I'm a basketball coach. The public can ask the basketball coach any question it wants; the man, however, is off limits. There's nothing in my contract that says I have to bare my soul to the media." A muscle in his jaw worked, betraying the vehemence behind his sober vow.

"Do you go by the strict letter of your contract? No give, here or there?" Her naturally inquisitive nature had taken over; the reporter had emerged, whether Daniel Strahan liked it or not.

He did not. His voice lowered, weighed down with tension. "Not when it comes to my personal life." His eyes were as dark as they'd been at the start; all warmth had vanished. "Tell me," he grew more pensive, "have *you* ever been interviewed?"

"Me?" She smiled, turning a slim forefinger on herself. "Uh-uh. I've always been on the other side of the notebook, thank goodness."

"You're relieved?"

"Yes," she answered quickly, then wised up to another trap. "I love *asking* questions. I love incorporating the answers into an intelligent piece."

"But suppose, just for the sake of argument, someone wanted to write a feature on a successful feature writer. How would you feel?"

Nia sensed the coiled readiness in her opponent and chose her words carefully. "If that successful feature writer was me? Very flattered."

The corner of his lip tightened at her evasion. "Would you give the interview?"

"That would depend on the soliciting publication."

"What if it were *Eastern Edge?*"

Nia couldn't help but begin to share his subtle

enjoyment of the verbal exchange. "I *work* for *Eastern Edge.* They'd never want to interview me."

His sigh was an exaggerated one. "Obviously. Take any other magazine of a similar caliber. Would you give the interview?"

"I don't know. I've never really thought about it."

"Well, think about it now. Would you?"

"I suppose it would hinge on the purpose of the feature."

The rhythm of the dialogue was broken by Daniel's silence. His eyes held hers, locked in wordless challenge. Nia was a willing captive, held prisoner by her own curiosity as much as by his visual command. He was certainly a far cry from the egocentric character she'd anticipated interviewing when Bill had first given her the assignment. There was a keen mind at work here and a depth of personality to be plumbed. But Nia sensed also that Daniel Strahan *would,* in fact, refuse her; that thought made her all the more determined.

"You really won't do it, will you?" she asked quietly.

He knew precisely what she was talking about. "No." He leaned an elbow on the arm of his chair and propped a fist against his jaw. It was a more nonchalant pose, more relaxed.

"Am I boring you?" she asked sweetly.

"No."

"You're not going to fall asleep on me, are you? I understand that, with the hectic schedules you fellows follow, you grab sleep whenever you can."

"Did David tell you that?"

It stunned her to realize that he must have. How else would she have known? Taking pity on her sudden alarm, Daniel ignored his own question as he shifted to a more attentive position.

"It's not necessarily true, at any rate. On the road, with midnight flights and periodic jet lag, your sleep schedule gets pretty messed up. The fellows often doze on the plane and take naps before games. But even though the schedule may be gruelling for the players, it's not necessarily hectic. There's a good deal of free time at every stop. That can be frustrating in itself."

"Free time? Is there?" she asked, unaware that her mask of detachment had slipped again to reveal her own past personal involvement.

"Sure." He scrutinized her sharply as he spoke in a low, even pitch. "Most games are played at night. During the day there may be a practice or a team meeting or a film of the team we'll be playing that night. But all told, there are hours at a stretch when each man is on his own."

Nia chewed the inside of her lip and frowned. That wasn't exactly the picture David had painted over the years. He had spoken of the nonstop life, the sheer exhaustion of the team, its sportswriter included. She had always assumed . . . but she knew better now. David's fatigue had been only in part a consequence of his work.

A sudden movement jarred her. Looking up quickly, she saw that Daniel had risen from his desk and approached her. Her eyes held the question he brusquely answered.

"Let's go. Interview's over." He seemed abruptly and inexplicably stern, as though his patience with the media had come to a sudden end. She half expected him to clamp his fingers around her arm and forcibly lead her from the room. It was a surprise when he gently took her coat from her lap and held it for her.

Slowly, she recovered, stood, and slid her arms carefully into the sleeves of the reefer. She was acutely aware of Daniel's tall presence behind her. His hands rested fleetingly on her shoulders before he stepped back.

Nia sent him a sheepish grin. "So I'm being kicked out?" She felt a light hand at her back and went with the movement toward the door.

"I'm hungry."

"What?"

"It's nearly one-thirty. Aren't *you* hungry?"

"Uh . . . I—I hadn't really thought about it," she stammered. She hadn't. If her stomach had growled, she'd been too engrossed in coping with Daniel Strahan to notice. "But I really should be getting back to the office."

Daniel guided her down the hallway, retracing the path she had taken earlier. "Then you won't have lunch with me?"

"Lunch?" Her gaze snapped sideways and up, focusing on the strong features of her escort.

"I do believe that's what we were discussing."

"We were discussing the demise of this interview."

"Let's discuss it over lunch."

"You mean," she asked, more hopeful in an instant, "that there's a chance you'll change your mind?"

He shook his head. "Nope."

They had reached the straightaway that led to the exit. Daniel paced his stride to more comfortably match hers, yet Nia still felt winded. Perhaps it was hunger, after all.

"Then what's the purpose of lunch?"

"I'm hungry." He held the door for her to pass.

"I don't think you need *me* to deal with *that,*" she taunted as she moved by, too late catching the double entendre. A hand on her arm halted her.

His voice was deeper, different. "I'd argue with you on that score if you weren't one of *them.* But I like to keep the press under my thumb, not in my bed. It's much safer that way."

For the first time Nia was aware of this man solely as a sexual being. As such, he was dangerous, dark and powerful. And his implication infuriated her. Throwing caution to the winds, she took the offense. "You take a lot for granted!" she seethed. "What makes you think I would jump into bed with you? Are you propositioned that often?"

His jaw tensed. "It has happened."

"Well," she said with a glare, "*I* don't work that way! I don't proposition men, for one thing. And, for another, you could no more get me near the game of basketball again than you could coax me into a pit of rattlers. I didn't want this assignment to begin with!"

From somewhere deep within she found the strength to pull her arm free of his grip. Driven by anger—at Daniel for having provoked her, at herself for having been provoked, and at Bill for having put her in the situation at all—she wheeled away and headed for her car at a fast clip. The March wind whipped at her hair, catching the edges of her coat and flaring them out to the sides. She had reached the car and was fumbling with the lock when the brass ring was taken from her fingers and those same fingers were enclosed in the pervading warmth of Daniel's hand.

"Let's take my car," he said, with a firmness that brooked no argument and a gentleness that precluded protest. To her astonishment Nia found herself being led toward, then tucked into, the front seat of a sporty Datsun 280Z. Not knowing quite what to say, she remained silent while Daniel circled the car and slid behind the wheel. His grace was an extension of the coordination she'd witnessed on the court earlier.

The purr of the motor was far smoother than her shaky mood. Staring out at the empty parking lot, she brooded. The self-satisfied, sexist overtone of his comment had rankled her, though she had to admit that her reaction had been unusually strong. What was it about Daniel Strahan that inspired such fire? Perhaps she felt threatened, she mused grudgingly; after all, he was more of a man than she'd come across in ages. Or was it the air of mystery about him?

They were on a back road headed west before Nia forced herself to speak. "Where are we going?"

"There's a small place not far from here where we can get something to eat. Italian. OK?" He spared a mere second to dart a glance at her, otherwise keeping his eyes glued to the road, and missed Nia's shrug.

"Why are you doing this?" she asked, calmed by the steady motion of the car and the passage of luxuriant greenery by the roadside.

"Taking you to lunch?" He paused. "I owe you."

Her head swung around. "For what?"

In profile, there was an angularity about him, from the even plane of his forehead beneath its brush of dark hair and the straight line of his nose to the firm set of his lips and the squared-off angle of his chin. "For failing to return your calls all week and causing you to make an unnecessary stop out here today. The least I can do is to feed you."

"Anything to keep the press happy, is that it?" she snapped, clinging to the last of her dissipating anger with something akin to survival instinct.

Again, he shot her a fast glance. "No. Actually, this is more person to person."

Better that than man to woman, she thought. "But aren't you afraid," she couldn't resist a jibe, "that in the course of a lunch you might inadvertently spill some little private tidbit that I'll greedily snatch up?"

"I trust you."

"Perhaps you shouldn't. I may be with *Eastern Edge* as an editor, but first and foremost I'm a writer. A reporter, if you will. Don't you know that reporters are slimy creatures who will seize upon anything for the sake of a story?"

"You wouldn't do that."

"Why not?"

"Because you're with *Eastern Edge,* for one

thing. That magazine doesn't print 'tidbits'; it only goes in for complete, well-planned and skillfully executed articles."

"If you believe that, why won't you agree to my interview?"

He showed no emotion. "Because I have nothing to say."

"God, are you stubborn!"

"No more so than you," he stated as fact.

"Then why in the world are we here?" Nia bristled. He had turned off the road and was now pulling up to a small group of stores, one of which was a charmingly sleepy-looking restaurant. "I didn't ask to be taken to lunch. You can easily turn around and take me back to my car."

Daniel angled the Datsun into a space, stilled its motor and uncoiled himself to step outside. When he reached Nia's side, opened her door and offered his hand, she took it. They were in the restaurant and seated opposite one another at a quiet booth before she was able to speak.

"I have no idea why I do it." She spoke half to herself, shaking her head in slow dismay. Her violet eyes clouded as they sought a solution.

Daniel frowned. "Do what?"

"Go right along with you . . . against my better judgment. It's happened three times now in the span of an hour." Her lips thinned. "I must be a masochist when it comes to men and basketball."

"Either that," his brown eyes warmed, "or you're as hungry as I am."

"*That* doesn't deserve an answer," she scolded softly, recalling all too vividly the problem they'd run into with double meanings earlier. Now she simply stared, awaiting Daniel's next move. If he wouldn't talk personally and she wouldn't talk shop, what was left?

The silence didn't bother him in the least. He studied her face for agonizingly long seconds before turning to gesture toward the waitress for two of something. It had been an hour of surprises for Nia; why not another? Dutifully, she refrained from asking what he'd ordered, pandering instead to more professional curiosity.

"Why *didn't* you return any of my calls?"

He glanced toward the ceiling. "Do you have any idea how many similar ones I get each week?"

"Do you ignore *all* of them?"

"No," he answered patiently, then lowered his head in an attitude of near mischief. "It just takes time to get around to returning them. I've found that the less interested ones lose interest after a week or two. They stop calling. That saves some of the dirty work."

"The dirty work being calling them back and refusing their requests?" she asked, feeling strangely defensive, almost guilty.

"Often."

Nia thought back to what he'd said earlier. "What about all that free time you mentioned? I would think you'd welcome the diversion, as a time-filler, if nothing else. It must be ego-boosting to grant a bevy of interviews."

"Ah," he breathed facetiously, "the professional athlete as an insufferable prima donna."

"Am I that far off-base?" She smiled in a challenge that Daniel Strahan met one-on-one.

"About me . . . yes. About some in the league . . . no. The game has changed dramatically over the last few years."

"Oh?" It was shaky ground for Nia, but she was hesitant to cut him off. There was always the possibility that, if she proved herself to be an innocuous, even pleasant companion, he might actually agree to her interview.

Daniel's explanation took the form of a pair of terse words. "Big money." His expression held a shadow of disdain.

"It's really changed things all that much?"

"Oh, yes," he drawled.

"How?"

As his gaze grew pensive, his fingers flexed, then intertwined. Nia looked down at them, noting both their length and latent strength. They were beautifully formed, begging to be explored and admired, one by one. Catching her breath at the thought, she forced her eyes up just in time to note Daniel's glimmer of awareness before it disappeared behind a mask of detachment.

He spoke quietly. "In the old days—"

"—when *you* played?" she teased him gently.

As though in punishment—or was it reward?—he grinned that honest to goodness grin of his, a grin that melted her own sense of detachment and left her struggling to recall the time and place. "Up until my last few playing years the pay was low and the benefits poor. Then the green came, mostly as a result of television." He leaned back when the waitress delivered a carafe of white wine and two crisp salads, then waited until she left to fill their glasses, one of which he raised in toast.

"To your stubborn streak."

Nia mimed his action with a grin. "To yours."

Both sipped before she prodded him on. "You were talking about television. . . ."

He nodded. "Do you know that, under league regulations, there must be at least two time-outs called in each period?" When she raised her eyebrows in question, he explained. "Commercials. The name of the game. And a source of millions. The team gets paid a hefty sum for the rights to televise its games. In turn, the players are treated as entertainers. Money. First-class accommodations. Numerous fringe benefits. Not to mention endorsements."

"Has the game itself suffered?" she asked, idly poking at her salad with a fork.

Daniel took a bite before answering. "I can't quite say that it has 'suffered.' 'Changed' is more accurate. Before the team functioned as a team; now the coaches find themselves with a group of individuals who have to be taught—and constantly reminded—to work together. There are many more rivalries and grudges, based solely on the fact that one player may be getting more money for doing a job another thinks is inferior to his own."

"Sounds touchy."

A deep laugh burst from the back of his throat. "It is. The modern coach is as much a diplomat as anything else."

"Do you enjoy it—coaching?"

He shrugged. "It puts bread on the table."

"Oh, come on," Nia charged lightly. "You have to feel more for it than *that.* In order to be good at what you do, you have to *love* it."

As if on cue, a basket of sliced Italian bread appeared. Daniel offered it to Nia, who shook her head in refusal, then helped himself to a slice and proceeded to butter it. She watched and waited, expecting some word on the extent of his emotional commitment. But he remained silent and all she saw was a self-confident man wise to her crafty conversational tactics. Acting on years of practice, he tossed the ball downcourt, straight toward the opposite basket.

"Do you love *your* work?" he asked, eyeing her over the rim of his wineglass.

"Uh-huh."

"Tell me about this feature."

"Yours?" Her eyes held pure innocence.

"No, Antonia," he chided with a smile. "The one you had *hoped* to snag me for."

Nia suddenly realized that she had no wish to tell him about the feature. She had too many doubts about it herself. Not to mention embarrassment. "Oh," she crinkled her nose, "you don't really want to hear about it. After all, if you're not interested in being part of it—"

"Tell me."

Her hesitation was awkward, made more so by the sheepish look she wore. Daniel saw it all. She finally opted for a vague elaboration. "It's a piece spotlighting several prominent easterners . . ."

"Prominent?" he asked, sensing more.

Nia wet her lips, then looked down. "Prominent and . . . and . . ."

"Well, what is it? Wealthy? Handsome? Dark-haired? Charming?"

"How about arrogant?" she shot back, pouting.

Daniel peered at her strangely. "You really *are* having trouble with this assignment, aren't you?" Her words, spoken in anger earlier, had come back to haunt her. There seemed no point in denial.

She threw her hands up as she spoke. "I think it's absurd! The ten most eligible easterners—it annoys me every time I think of it!"

"The ten most eligible easterners?" he echoed in disbelief. "In *Eastern Edge?*"

"That's what *I* said." She grimaced. "But Bill was adamant. Have you ever heard anything so foolish?"

Daniel never got a chance to respond for, at that moment, their lunch was set quietly before them. It was an attractive dish—thin-sliced veal in a light cream sauce, with a vegetable potpourri that included eggplant, zucchini, peppers and several other goodies. "Thanks, Sue." He smiled up at the waitress, who blushed and left without a word.

"Do you eat here often?" Nia asked, wondering at the familiarity. He hadn't even bothered to look at a menu, yet a magnificent presentation had been made. Its smell was divine.

"Oh, several times a week—when we're home. I don't live far from here . . . and I'm not a terribly good cook. This is the special of the day. Is it all right for you?"

"It's fine. It's lovely! I'm just amazed. I mean,

where's all the backslapping and handshaking and basketball talk from the owners and other patrons?"

His gaze narrowed. "If I found that here I'd never come back. The owner knows that. It's bad enough when you walk through airports or into elegant restaurants and someone recognizes you. It doesn't matter how hungry or tired or rushed you may be—the public *expects.* That's why I eat here. These people *don't.* And," he paused, lowering his voice, "that's another reason I won't let you write about me. I *need* my privacy."

The force of his declaration led to a short span of quiet, during which they began to eat. Nia reflected on his feelings, wondering in particular about that privacy he prized so highly.

"Why *are* you 'eligible' . . . Daniel?" Her question in part related to her use of his name, which felt pleasantly comfortable on her tongue.

His smile proved the rightness of it. "Yes, Daniel. And why am I 'eligible'? I suppose because I'm not married."

"I did manage to guess that," she quipped facetiously. "But why not?"

He shrugged off the importance of the question. "It doesn't suit my lifestyle."

"Have you *ever* been married?"

He ignored her, proceeding to eat in silence for a minute. "This is beginning to sound suspiciously like an interview."

"It isn't," she rebounded quickly. "I'm curious."

"Naturally."

"It *is* odd to find someone like you without a

steady companion. If for no other purpose than to cook you private dinners . . ."

Daniel put down his fork. "The kind of woman who would interest me would have to be both intelligent and independent. Do you honestly think that *that* kind of woman would be content to sit around my house waiting for me to return at odd hours and odd days?"

"If she loved you, she might."

"I'd *never* ask a woman to do that. It's a cruel life for a married couple. You, of all people, should know that!"

Nia flinched. "A low blow," she murmured, twisting her locket self-consciously. "But the blame was David's and mine."

"Is that why you despise the entire game of basketball?"

"I don't. It's just . . . just that . . . anything to do with basketball brings back painful memories." She frowned, lifted her wineglass and sipped from it absently, then replaced it on the table and took a deep breath. "I should be over it by now," she whispered, wishing she was, fearing that this man's company complicated the issue in more ways than one. Not only was he a vital part of the world she'd religiously avoided over the years, but she had to admit that, quite involuntarily, she found him very attractive.

"How long has it been?" His gentle voice was soothing, another facet of that lure. Had he been boorish and uncouth, she might easily have lumped him together with her other reasons for disliking the sport. But he appeared to be intelligent, a true thinking man. For some reason, she felt that he could affect her emotions.

"Just about five years." She faced him with a mustering of her poise. "We were married for nearly another five, most of which were difficult."

"You *were* much younger than David, weren't you?"

"Uh-huh. Fifteen years, to be exact." It seemed perfectly normal to be talking with Daniel this way. There was a strength about him that inspired confession; he was like an old friend, content to listen. "But . . . the age difference was only secondary in our troubles."

"Oh?"

The layers of her dark hair shimmied with her headshake. "We couldn't coordinate our lives. We went in different directions, physically *and* emotionally."

"Then it wasn't just . . . the women . . . ?"

Nia smiled sadly. "You don't mince words, do you?" At Daniel's silent shrug, she was bidden to answer his question. "No," she sighed. "Much as I'd like to believe differently, the infidelity was only part of it. I needed a husband, someone to *be* there, to share life with. All David needed was his column . . . and basketball."

They ate in silence for several moments. Daniel reflected on what she'd told him, wondering about the parallels to his own life and needs. Nia considered her own thoughts and her astonishment at having shared them so freely. But here was a man who prized his confidentialities; surely he would respect hers. She felt sure that her confessions would go no further than this booth.

"Do you ever see him?" Daniel asked at last, sitting back to digest his lunch.

Nia grunted. "I should ask *you* that. He must cover the games you play against the Spurs."

"Yes, I do see him when we're in San Antonio. Our relationship is strictly a business one." He paused, his brown-eyed gaze softening even before he posed his question. "Do you miss him?"

"No."

"You're very sure."

"I am."

"Do you live alone?"

"Yes."

"Lonely?"

Her gaze was shuttered as she caught her breath, then she peered through her lashes at him. A blend of hesitance and humor lowered her voice to a vague imitation of his. "This is beginning to sound suspiciously like an interview."

"It isn't." He smiled, recalling and echoing her earlier riposte. "I'm just curious."

"About *me?"* It was worth a try to divert him; he was far too comfortable a companion. She needed a sharp reminder of who he was and why she was with him. "I've got nothing to offer. *You're* the one with the secret life. *You're* the one the public wants to hear about. Come on, Daniel. I'd really like to do that interview."

His state of gentle relaxation became a thing of the past. As he stiffened, he raised two fingers to the waitress who instantly brought hot coffee. Nia watched him closely, bemused by his abrupt mood change and strangely sad to bid his friendly side good-bye. It was as though her reminder of who *he* was had triggered his remembrance of *her* affiliation. It was a necessary progression of events; after all, he'd be headed back to the arena, while she'd be aimed for Boston and the offices of *Eastern Edge.*

"Oh, no," she exclaimed, suddenly mindful of the fact that she'd been expected back in the office much earlier. "I've got to make a phone call. Is there a pay phone here?"

He stretched, dug his hand into the pocket of his slacks, and presented her with a quarter. "Out back."

Nia stared at the quarter. "What's that for?" she asked, her own wallet in her hand as she slid out of the booth.

"Your call."

"I have change."

"Use it," he ordered in a voice that resembled the one he'd used to command his players at the practice earlier. His expression was taut; Nia had no wish to goad him further.

Taking the quarter, she escaped to the back of the restaurant. Her mind was suddenly a jumble in anticipation of Bill Austen's anger at their missed meeting, his skepticism when she'd have to tell him that Daniel Strahan had refused her request, Daniel's own tightness on the entire subject. With so many legitimate sources of worry, why was she fixated on such a petty matter as the intimate warmth of the small coin that Daniel had taken from his thigh pocket?

Scowling in self-reproach, she put through her call, apologizing as best she could to Bill, putting as much of the blame for her delay as she could on Daniel.

"He's giving me a really hard time, Bill." She spoke softly to avoid being overheard. "I don't think he'll agree to it." Might as well warn the boss ahead of time.

But the voice on the other end of the line was far from sympathetic. "Convince him, Nia. You can do it if anyone can. Be wily. Be feminine. Get to him."

"Do you have any idea what you're asking?" she bit back in dismay.

Bill's return was sharp. "I'm not asking you to do anything but be persuasive. I know that you're not eager to do this assignment. But I do want you to give it your best before you give up on that one."

"*That one* is a very stubborn man," she argued. Why did she feel like a traitor saying such a thing?

"Well, *you* be stubborn, too!" he snapped, jolting her into recollecting the toast she and Daniel had so recently exchanged. "And get yourself back here before the day is a total waste, Nia. If we don't go over this collegiate piece we'll never get it to the printer for next month's issue! We've got to do it today!"

"I know," she breathed. "I know. I'll be there within the hour." After replacing the receiver, she rested her forehead on the wall mount. Some days, nothing came easily. . . .

"Is everything all right?"

Nia jerked her head up in surprise to find Daniel standing beneath the archway that led to the small alcove which housed the phone. He had thrust his hands into the pockets of his pants, of necessity forcing aside the front of his blazer to reveal a broad expanse of shirt-sheathed chest. Oh, he *was* attractive. . . .

"Uh . . . yes . . ." she began, then changed her tune as indignation set in. "No!" she gritted quietly. "Everything's *not* all right! My boss is furious that I'm late—we were supposed to go over some things together this afternoon. By the time I get back into town there'll be barely enough time to do anything. He doesn't care that *you* shanghaied me into having lunch with you. An intimate little lunch," she scoffed, tossing her head back. "The only one who's been at all intimate is *me.*" Her eyes flashed with violet fury. "If we had more time I might well have been duped into telling you my whole life's story! What I can't understand is how you managed to get me to talk—when I can't even get you to *consider* returning the favor."

The unevenness of her breathing was a direct result of her tightly bridled anger. She was acutely aware of where they were; had it been a more private location, she would have lashed out more loudly. Now, she simply stood and glared.

Throughout the softly seething barrage, Daniel hadn't budged. Now he didn't say a word until she had remained silent for a full minute.

"Are you done?" he asked calmly, his thoughts on her outburst well hidden behind a civil veneer.

"Yes!"

"Then let's get out of here." Straightening, he turned and led the way.

three

THE SHORT RETURN TRIP WAS MADE IN SI-lence. She stared out the side window, a fist jammed against her chin. His eyes never left the road. When the arena loomed before them, Daniel pulled up beside her car.

Nia's eyes dropped to her lap and she bolstered herself with a deep breath. "Look, Daniel, I'm sorry I went on that way. It was wrong of me."

"Wrong to speak your mind?" His voice was smooth, in control.

Innate honesty brought her head up, her gaze to his. "Wrong to take *my* frustration out on you. I'm sure that you've got your share of aggravation. Besides, you were right, back there in your office. *You* didn't ask me to come here. For that matter, you didn't ask to be chosen by *Eastern Edge* for its feature. I'm sorry if I've spoiled your free time . . . and your lunch."

Daniel sat back against the rich leather of the

bucket seat, stared forward for a minute, then glanced toward Nia. "You didn't do that." There was a deeper thread in his voice, one she might have ignored had it not been for the darker glint in his eye. Nia grew more conscious of the intimacy of the car and the long, lean example of masculinity beside her. For all her anger at him, she couldn't deny the powerful draw of the man. He was a mass of good looks and subtle sensuality, kindling feelings within her that she simply couldn't face.

Cursing her own vulnerability, she tugged at the handle of the door, swearing softly when it wouldn't give. The long arm that reached across her solved that problem with the flick of the lock, even as its nearness temporarily halted her flight. It recoiled slowly, retracing a path that skimmed her middle beneath her breasts. Its heat was vivid despite the layers of her sweater and coat.

Nia caught her breath, wavered, then made her escape, only to be stopped once more at her own car by the deep voice that called to her, its sound easily besting the brisk breeze.

"I'll consider it."

Fearing she'd misheard him, Nia turned slowly. The sleek maroon body of Daniel's car stood between them; his arm was outstretched on its roof. Now that he had her attention, he moved more leisurely around the car and came to stand before her.

"I'll consider it," he repeated, raising both palms toward her in a gesture of peace. "I can't promise that I'll agree, but I *will* think about it."

Skepticism brought a frown to Nia's gentle features, yet words eluded her. She felt confused, torn between regarding Daniel as a superb sportsman . . . or simply a superb man. Unsure, she pondered the choice as she distractedly unlocked her own door and slid into the driver's seat. The slam of the door was a shot of encouragement; the token barrier was better than none. On impulse, she rolled down her window and squinted back up at Daniel, whose dark head was haloed by the afternoon sun.

"You will?" she asked in childlike disbelief.

He nodded, bending to bring his face closer. "I will." The glint had become a gleam, fascinating Nia into lingering.

"And . . . to what do I owe this change of heart?" She smiled more coyly than she had as yet. The quiet ring of her own voice, softer and more feminine, gave her the answer she sought. Her smile faded as her heart skipped a beat. *Start the car,* a tiny voice cried, but she was unable to move. Daniel's eyes released her gaze only to fall to the lower lip she unknowingly chewed. Her eyes widened in uncharacteristic fear. This wasn't what she wanted. It was far too dangerous. Daniel Strahan was too attractive a man; she shouldn't play with this kind of fire.

"Don't," she whispered, condensing her protest into one word of sanity.

But Daniel silently overrode her objection, lowering his head until his face was close, so close. Once again she protested, shaking her head in slow denial of the force that seemed destined to draw them together. His warmth reached out to her, holding her suddenly still as he moved a fraction of an inch until his lips touched hers. The sweetness of his kiss overwhelmed her. It was light and gentle, dealing with her fear by tantalizing her with a wisp of a caress that left tingles at every touchpoint. She gasped when he drew back, but he kissed her again, as lightly as before and as briefly. Her lips felt cool when he left them once more, this time to take in the flush on her cheeks and the nascent light of desire in her eyes.

His taunting had done its job, leaving her aware and receptive. She offered no resistance when his lips lowered a third time, meeting hers fully and with a persuasive power that set her senses reeling. The gentle command of his kiss had ensured her commitment; her response was inevitable.

Slowly, Nia opened to him, with an involvement she hadn't shown in years. She was curious, as interested in the depth of his virility as he was in her abandonment. Staking his claim, he deepened the kiss. If this was the first offering of his personal stock, she savored it fully. Eyes closed, she drank in the heady taste of his mouth, a taste tinged with the memory of coffee laced with cream and four sugars. Sensing her pleasure, he offered more, sampling the moistness of her mouth with the tip of his tongue. A tremor of sheer delight sizzled its way through her.

Suddenly a raucous call, a shout, a long and suggestive whistle tore them apart, shattering the moment with an abrupt return to reality.

"Not bad, coach . . . !"

"Go get her, man!"

"Heeeey, Professor . . . At-a-way . . . !"

Releasing her lips with a shuddering moan, Daniel slowly straightened. His eyes held Nia's for an instant of silent apology before he turned his head to glare at the three Breakers sauntering across the parking lot. The first thing Nia noted was their superior height; as had been obvious at the practice that morning, they towered over Daniel. The second, and far more startling, thing she noted was their response to the coach. He said nothing, simply stared at them, his hands cocked ominously on his hips. As though physically lashed, they shied away and hastened toward a waiting car, slithering in with a tangle of arms and legs, then belatedly minding their own business as the car sped off. It was an impressive show—this power of Daniel's—but one that was consistent with the more private showing she'd had moments before. Nia was rudely awakened to her folly.

When Daniel turned back and opened his mouth to speak she held out a hand to silence him. This time, when she shook her head, he kept his distance. Her distress was obvious.

"I've got to go," she whispered hoarsely; starting the car and backing out of the space, she drove out of the parking lot without a look back. More than anything, she needed to think. The cool air rushed in through her open window, gradually calming her senses and clearing her head. She had all of twenty minutes of travel time to make sense out of what had happened.

Of the emotions that whirled about her mind,

self-reproach took the lead. For the first time in her professional career, she had truly blown it! Oh, yes, Daniel Strahan had said that he'd consider her request. But would he really ever consent to the interview? No! She knew it in her heart.

And, in her heart, she couldn't really blame him. In her heart, she didn't *want* him to give in. For she *did* believe him to be a very private person; he'd convinced her of that in deed as well as in word. To hound him further would be to violate something totally unexpected and surprisingly precious—her respect for him as a human being.

In the course of her years as a writer Nia had come to rely on instinct in judging her quarry. Rarely were her first impressions wrong—exaggerated or understated, perhaps, but rarely wrong. Today, Daniel Strahan had struck her as a man of character, of dedication, of honesty. One part of her was reluctant to share him. And *that* was the crux of her dilemma.

He had kissed her. She had kissed him back. By all reasonable estimates, she had broken the very first rule in the book. Hadn't *she* been the one to lash out at Daniel when he'd spoken of "hunger" in such a seductive vein? Yet she had melted beneath his touch, offering little more than token resistance. In the matter of a few short hours she had ceased to view him as a subject and had begun to view him as a man. Tall. Virile. Compelling. But he was a *basketball* star. *How could she have done it?*

The torrent of dismay tossed her one step ahead. There was no possible future with a man like Daniel, regardless of the strength of his appeal.

He'd said as much himself; his lifestyle wreaked havoc with relationships. *She should know.*

So, if a relationship was out of the question, what *had* been the justification for that kiss? Aside from the sheer pleasure of the moment, there seemed to be none. And *that* was quite out of character. The need for physical experimentation had exhausted itself in Nia's marriage. Yes, she dated often, but raw physical desire had never played a part in her social life since the divorce. What had happened today?

The turnpike curved to the right and crested a rise, bringing the skyline of Boston into full view. Its sight was instantly comforting to Nia, as was the landscape of Cambridge to her left. This was home. Its nearness reassured her; its life enveloped her. By the time she had left the pike and negotiated the downtown streets she felt nearly normal. There was still the unfinished business of the eligible easterner feature that had caused her trouble from the start. But there were other things to think of, more immediate things. Daniel Strahan could wait his turn.

Daniel Strahan, however, was not one to wait. He *made* his turn, taking the offensive, stealing the ball on the rebound and breaking fast with it. Nia scarcely had time to settle into a chair by Bill Austen's desk when the phone rang.

"Yes," Bill clipped absently, then shot a glance at Nia. Both brows lifted in speculation, he held out the receiver.

Startled, she took it. "Hello?"

"Antonia . . . ? It's Dan." How could she ever forget that voice? "Are you . . . all right?"

For the past ten minutes, she'd been able to divert her mind from the embarrassment she felt. Now it was all back. With an audience, no less. Was she all right? If self-reproach, frustration and guilt were the normal state of things, she was fine.

"Dan who?" she quipped, unable to resist the barb. But her voice was soft and a far cry from the expression of annoyance she'd intended.

"Ahhh. She *is* all right." He spoke slowly, deeply. Nia tried to picture him in his office, balanced back in his chair, half buried in a world she could never share. Unfortunately, the man stood out in her mind, tall and alluring. She heard the smile in his voice. "And sweet as ever."

"As ever."

He paused for a minute. "Are you angry?"

"Hmmph." She looked up to catch Bill's sharpened gaze, then quickly averted her eyes, lowered her head, and turned from him to perch on the corner of his desk.

"At *me?*" Momentary wariness came low over the wire.

"Among others."

"At my . . . wards?"

"They're charming," she offered in quiet sarcasm.

Daniel hesitated, then plunged. "At yourself?"

"Bingo." Unconsciously, she put her little finger against the tight coil of the phone wire and began to work it around.

"Well, don't be. It takes two, you know."

"Tell me."

"It takes two."

Nia bit her lip in a bid for patience. Bill shifted in his seat and Daniel, miraculously, saw it all.

"Your boss is right there?"

"Uh-huh." And he was eyeing her very strangely.

"Well, tell him I'm thinking about it."

"You'll never do it." The tip of her finger was all but hidden in the white coil.

"I may."

"I doubt it."

"Don't you want me to?"

She tucked her chin more tightly against her chest, so that her voice was nearly muffled. "No." The resultant pause was predictable.

"Now . . . that *does* surprise me. Was the decision made before . . . or after . . . we met?"

"A little of both." Bill's restlessness was a glaring hint from the corner of her eye. "Listen," she half whispered, "I've got to run."

"OK. Be good." He accepted the brush-off without a fuss.

"You, too." The receiver had already left her ear when his parting shot brought it quickly back.

"Will you be watching the game tonight?"

"No."

"Why don't you try."

"Uh-uh." The first joint of her pinkie had disappeared as well now.

"It might be helpful . . . if you hope to write that article."

"I don't."

"You may."

"It's not about the game."

"Ahhh. That's right. It's about me. But . . . is there really a distinction?"

Her voice rose for the first time, fraught with urgency. "Yes! You know there is!"

Again, she heard his smile, could almost see it dancing at the corners of his firm lips. "Just as long as *you* do, too. Take care." And he hung up, leaving her to stare dumbly at the receiver. It was Bill's firm hand that relieved her of the burden, replacing it on its cradle as she fumbled to free her finger from the cord. Her head was still down when Bill confronted her.

"What was *that* all about?"

The instant her gaze met his, she knew that deception would be a waste of time. If there was to be a new man in the number five slot for the eligible eastern men article, Bill Austen might as well know now.

"*That* was Daniel Strahan."

Bill's initial surprise quickly gave way to perception. "Uh-oh."

She grimaced. "Uh-oh is right! He won't do it."

"An out-and-out no?"

Again, she couldn't lie. "Well, he said he'd consider it. But after spending the better part of two hours with the man, I can tell you that he won't do it."

"Even after you spoke to me, you couldn't convince him?"

"*Especially* then." Her mind's eye replayed

those concluding minutes and her cheeks warmed, quite against her will. Bill was all too aware of the flush. Strolling to the far side of the room, ostensibly to study the assignment board, he hid his expression from her.

"Was today the first time you've met the man?"

"Yes."

He lifted a hand to stroke his jaw. "That's interesting."

"What is?" she countered on impulse, sensing his drift only when he turned back to face her.

"That . . . conversation you just had with him." He darted an insinuating glance at the phone. "I would have thought you were talking with an old friend, perhaps a lover . . . despite that 'Dan who?' you threw out at the start."

Nia's blush deepened with her consternation. "He's not an old friend *or* a lover. But he does have this . . . way . . . of getting to you."

"To *you,* perhaps. Not *me.* That was very definitely a feminine response he drew from you just now."

"Then *you* interview him, Bill," she implored gently, desperately. "I've had problems with this one from the first. If you feel that I'm too susceptible to him, *you* do it. You know how I feel about anything to do with basketball."

It wasn't often that Bill Austen, or anyone at *Eastern Edge,* for that matter, saw Nia Phillips quite so disturbed. Taking momentary pity on her plight, he spoke more kindly. "Still that bad?"

"Uh-huh." She emphasized each syllable with suitable disgust.

"But you did like Strahan . . . as a person?"

Nia could see the wheels of his mind turning and didn't like their direction. "Bill . . ."

Sympathy was a thing of the past; Bill had reached his decision. "Stick with it, Nia. Just a little longer. See if you can get him to come around."

"Bill," she readied for the fight, "I don't think—"

"Now, about this collegiate item." He cast a pointed look at his watch. "We've got an hour to get it downstairs."

Courting danger, she stared at him, then shook her head and sighed, suddenly tired. Nothing had been settled, but at least Bill knew where she stood. When the Strahan interview fell through, as she was sure it would, she would have given Bill fair warning. If they were pinched at the last minute in finding a replacement, it wouldn't be *her* fault. If Bill was content to let the matter ride for the time being, so was she. Unfortunately, it wasn't that simple.

Daniel Strahan was a bug in her ear, impossible to dislodge. She found herself thinking about him that night as she drove home in the dark, across the Charles River to her Cambridge home. *Had* he called her from the arena? Or had he been at home? Where was home—in Weston, as he had implied? *What* was home—a house, an apartment, a condominium? Surely he was at the arena now; the game would be starting within the half hour. Was he, at this moment, preparing to face the press?

Nia lived in an older, quiet section, on a residential street just beyond the central Harvard University crush. Most days she walked the ten minutes into the square, hopped the rapid transit, and was downtown in a matter of another ten or fifteen minutes. If it rained, she could get a bus at the end of her street. On days like today, with appointments away from Boston, she took her car.

Pulling into the gravel drive of the two-family house, she parked alongside the battered Volvo owned by her tenant, Frederick Maxwell. Dr. Max, as he was affectionately called by the academic community, was professor emeritus in history at Harvard. A remarkable man despite his almost eighty years, he went to "work" every day, spending hours reading and gathering his thoughts for the masterpiece he still planned to write. Friends and colleagues indulged him both his eccentricities and his age, picking up papers he unknowingly dropped in his shuffle down the hall, flipping light switches off after him, seeing that the tail end of his car was tucked safely alongside the curb.

Now Nia smiled as she stepped from her own car to turn off the headlights Dr. Max had left on, saving him the hassle of a dead battery the next morning. As his landlord and friend, she was glad to do things for the old man whenever she could, though his pride and determination kept him from asking. He had lived in the house when she and David had bought it ten years ago; he was as unobtrusive a tenant as one could hope to have.

Briefcase in hand, shoulder bag in place, she climbed the porch steps and unlocked her front door. From the lower apartment came the faint sound of the evening news. It was a noise akin to the occasional distant siren, one she had easily learned to ignore. On this night, however, it sparked thoughts of another program shortly to go on the air. He had asked her to watch the game; should she? The very thought sent ripples of tension through her, a purely reflexive response conditioned by years of waiting and wondering. David had never wished to include her in his professional life, preferring that she remain at home on the grounds that he was working and couldn't be distracted. On occasion she'd turned on the television set to catch sight of him; finally, she gave that up as well and sought refuge in her own life, gradually basing a full-time career on her writing skill. Eventually she had no time to watch televised games . . . much less the desire to do so.

Kneeling gracefully, she scooped up the mail from the floor and thumbed through the pile as she mounted the stairs. One more key in the lock at the top and she was home free.

Her briefcase and bag landed softly on a chair as she passed through the living room; the mail sailed on to the dining room table. Shrugging out of her coat, she hung it in the hall closet, then proceeded to her room to change.

Within minutes she was barefoot, wearing jeans and a turtleneck sweater, rummaging through the contents of the freezer for the steak she was sure remained. Then she paused, closed the freezer, opened the lower refrigerator door and extracted two eggs and a slice of American cheese. A simple omelet would be all she'd need, what with the large lunch she'd had with Daniel.

Daniel. Her eye flew to the small television set

propped at the end of the kitchen bar. She rarely watched, save for the news, and then only if she happened to be eating at the time. Her slim gold watch read seven twenty-five. Nearly time for the opening jump-off. Would the pregame interviews be over? Would Daniel be back at his bench by now?

Gnawing on that same overworked lower lip, she fished a frying pan from the cabinet, dug for the butter, then put them both down with a muffled curse. Her arm snaked toward the television, her fingers turned the knob to "on," then roughly twisted the channel selector until she hit on the proper one.

The arena was darkened; the spotlight was at mid-court. Standing reverently atop the blue Breaker emblem was a dark-haired woman with a mike. Relative silence prevailed for an instant, to be broken by the woman's rich soprano as she sang the national anthem.

Nia slowly exhaled the breath she'd been holding, flicked the switch to an unpatriotic "off," and slumped against the high wooden stool by the counter. She had missed the pregame interviews. The game itself was about to begin. *That* wasn't what interested her. Rather, it was Daniel. Why had she hesitated? Why hadn't she turned the set on sooner? Had it been pure stubbornness on her part? Even arrogance? Then why was she disappointed now?

It occurred to her that she would very much have liked to have seen him on the air. Their lunch together had given her a glimpse of him off-court, even though he had been studiously close-mouthed about his private life. What was he like in his official capacity as head coach of the New England Breakers?

Well, she acknowledged with a drawn-out sigh, she'd blown it again. Twice in one day . . . poor show. Better to chalk this day off and move on. After all, Daniel Strahan was nothing more than an assignment, was he not? When he called to give his final "no," they would have no more to do with one another.

So she reminded herself at intervals all evening, each time she took a break from her reading. Her attention was supposedly focused on the Amish feature for which she was scheduled to travel to Pennsylvania the following week. This preliminary work was imperative if she hoped to make maximum use of her time in the field.

With the spate of interruptions that characterized life in the office, she often saved such reading for home. Tonight, however, the interruptions were of her own making. Was it half-time? Was it over? Had he won? Or lost? Was the locker room aswarm with reporters devouring his postgame comments? Had he left? Where was he now? What did a coach do when the stadium emptied and the lights went out? What did *Daniel Strahan* do?

Breakers Topple Bullets, 112–94. The triumphant words exploded from the sports page the following morning, hitting Nia in the face as she peered over the shoulder of a man on the subway. Chivalry had vanished with the quarter token. This stranger sat; Nia stood. She had no qualms at all about reading his paper.

They had won. Ten in a row. Not bad. Perhaps, riding high on this string of victories, Daniel might be favorably disposed to grant her the interview. Once again she wondered whether that was what she wanted. But it was out of her hands; it was *his* decision now. When would he contact her?

It happened when she least expected it. She was tired and just the slightest bit miffed at the thought that, given the extent of her own preoccupation with the man and this assignment, he should not be conscientious in reaching a decision.

The subway was particularly crowded on her way home, the crowd particularly restless. When Nia reached the square she peered from the kiosk at the pouring rain that had not been forecast . . . and the bus that had just pulled away from the curb and sailed down Brattle Street oblivious to her plight.

A treat. That was what she needed. It would be a good ten minutes before the next bus rolled in. Ten minutes. In silent calculation, she looked toward The Lobster's Claw at the far end of a side street. Did she have time? Did she have enough cash? Could she make it there and back without a total drenching?

On impulse she made the break, darting from doorway to doorway until she reached her destination, returning in similarly sporadic fashion with a half-pound of fresh-cooked lobster meat tucked safely beneath her arm.

As though on command, the bus appeared. Boarding quickly, she savored its warm, dry haven, if only for the few minutes' ride to the top of her street. Anticipation of the gastronomical treasure she carried lightened her gait as she ran down the street and up her front steps. It was there that she found Daniel.

four

THE RELENTLESS SPATTER OF THE RAIN masked the extent of her alarm at finding a tall interloper on her dark front porch. It took her a minute to catch her breath.

"Daniel!" she cried. "You frightened me."

The dull glow of the nearby streetlamp illuminated his damp khaki trenchcoat. "I'm sorry. I was about to leave when I saw you running down the street. Where's your umbrella?"

She cocked her head toward the door. "Inside. Keeping the hall closet dry."

His face was in the shadow of the overhanging roof, but Nia could feel his wry smile. "Makes sense. Have you got a key?"

Groping in her pocket for the large brass ring, she handed it to him. "The yellow one."

"You can see it in the dark?"

"Yes."

So did he, quickly singling out the key with the

rubber identifying ring glowing yellow around its head. As soon as the door was opened Nia rushed inside, shaking the rain from her sleeves as she flipped on the light and climbed the stairs.

"Next one's green," she called over her shoulder. Directly behind her, Daniel skimmed the key ring, found the proper one, and let them, at last, into her home. Dropping her things onto a chair and draping her sodden coat over its back, Nia ran her fingers through the dampness of her hair, then turned to face Daniel. Having taken her lead, he had thrown his own coat over a chair to dry. Now he stood across the room, with two chairs, a sofa, and a glass coffee table as buffers between them. He looked unconscionably handsome in a gray tweed blazer and darker charcoal slacks. His black vee-neck sweater contrasted with the white of his oxford cloth shirt, both extremes tempered by the very gentle expression he wore.

For an instant Nia didn't know what to say. Was this a business call . . . or a personal one? "I . . . I never expected to find you *here.*" She finally forced herself to break the vibrant silence.

"I tried calling," he explained softly. "There was no answer, so I thought I'd take a ride over."

She smiled shyly, tucking a wisp of hair behind her ear. "Lovely weather you brought."

"How far did you have to walk?"

At the mention of walking she grew suddenly aware of her wet feet. Without thought of the consequence, she stepped out of her shoes and knelt to pick them up. It was only when she straightened that she realized the disadvantage she had unwittingly emphasized. At five eight she was above average in height and willowy, but flat-footed before this man she was nearly petite.

"Uh . . . it wasn't far. Just from the top of the street."

"I'm sorry." He offered a second apology, though he neither moved nor looked away. "If I'd known, I could have picked you up there."

"No problem." She scoffed away its import with a crinkle of her nose, all the while wondering where they were to go from here. "How . . . how did you know where I live?"

He shrugged. "The book."

"The phone book? There must be at least eight A. Phillipses listed."

The corner of his mouth quirked knowingly. "Six. Three in Cambridge, two in Boston, one in Charlestown."

He stood with one hand in his slacks pocket, the other hanging casually by his side. On the surface he was relaxed, yet Nia couldn't help but sense his alertness. Was he, too, recalling their last meeting and its finale?

"You stopped at the other two Cambridge addresses?" She pursued the potentially inane line of questioning only for lack of sure footing. Her ground was truly shaky when it came to Daniel Strahan.

His smile spread in slow accompaniment to his approach. "No," he crooned, rounding the sofa to stand before her. "I checked with *our* book."

His proximity forced her to look more sharply up. "*Your* book?"

"The one kept by the PR man with names, addresses and phone numbers of, among others, the sportswriters. This address may have been crossed out, but it was still legible."

"I see." So the contact had indirectly been traceable to David. How fitting. And ominous. "No game tonight?" she asked more coolly, partly in defense of his nearness, of which she was acutely aware.

Daniel raised a chiding brow. "We can't play *every* night. The schedule is exhausting for the players as it is."

"A shame," she mused, feeling little sympathy at the moment, knowing only her need to put space between them. He *was* handsome. She could feel the magnetism of his masculinity and was frightened. "Look, would you excuse me?" She grimaced at her spattered stockings. "I'd really like to change into dry things." If it was a subtle invitation for him to leave, he promptly overlooked it.

"I was hoping to take you to dinner."

"You were?" She peered up at him, half-skeptical, half-pleased. Again her pulse skipped—was it work or play?

Daniel's expression remained calm and controlled, giving nothing away. "Can I tempt you?"

"No."

"No?" He was obviously taken aback by the bluntness of her rejection. "Why not?" he asked, but without indignance.

"Because I've already made dinner plans." She glanced toward the chair where she'd dropped her bundle, just as he glanced at his watch.

"You have a date?"

"No. I'm staying in. There's no way I'm going back out in *that* rain!" Natural impetuosity had taken over for a minute, leaving Nia's caution behind. "I've got my dinner planned here."

"Oh," he said baldly, not quite understanding. "You're eating alone?"

It was the odd and unexpected note of regret in his voice that restored her own composure fully. Her mind on the lobster meat, she grinned. "I had planned to."

With a silent nod he looked away, back toward his coat, as though wishing he didn't have to go back out into the torrent either. In that moment something struck Nia—something strangely akin to a fleeting glimmer of loneliness in Daniel's mien—and she was touched.

"You can join me if you'd like," she burst out on the spur of the moment. Her tone had that same soft, feminine lilt that Bill had commented on the day before. It also held sincerity; she wanted him to stay.

His dark head turned back cautiously. "You've got enough?"

She smiled freely, already envisioning the meal. "I think I can scrounge something up. But first," she scowled in mock upset, "I've *got* to change." Without another word she escaped to her room, closing the door behind her and stripping off her skirt and blouse to climb into jeans, a sweater and moccasins. Despite the discrepancy in their height she felt suddenly stubborn. If Daniel Strahan planned to eat here, he'd do it on *her* terms. She wore frills and high heels all day long; at night, she deserved a respite.

Taking a towel to her damp hair, she rubbed it vigorously, then went to work with a brush, coaxing the multiple layers into a semblance of glorious mahogany order. With a final touch of blusher and a dab of pale apple lip gloss, she stood back to survey the end result.

Her mirror reflected a comely sight. She was slender but shapely, the gentle swell of her breasts creating the feminine effect denied by the slim stretch of her straight-legged jeans. Her hair, at its longest, fell to her shoulders, its soft layering gentling her sculpted features. Of the latter, it was her eyes that dominated, violet, and gay now as they hadn't been in a very long time.

For an instant Nia frowned at herself. What *was* she doing? But, damn it, she had her lonely times, too. Was it wrong to share dinner with a . . . a . . . a friend?

When Nia returned to the living room Daniel was not there. Reaching down for the package of lobster meat, she heard a noise in the kitchen, a noise that instinctively brought crushing and infuriating thoughts to her mind. Fuelled by dismay, she ran toward the kitchen, only to find her guest calmly rummaging through the drawer in search of a corkscrew with which to open the bottle of wine he'd removed from the counter rack.

"Oh!" she gasped in relief, a hand on her chest to ease her breathlessness. "I thought you were at the television set." Her gaze narrowed in warning.

"If you have any intention of watching a basketball game from *this* house, you can just forget it." As he closed the drawer and came toward her, she blustered on, determined to make her point. "There is *no* basketball here—high school, college *or* professional. Got that?"

Before she could gather her senses, much less her scattered wits, Daniel raised his hands to her face. His fingers slid into her hair, their length curving to fit her head. His eyes held a spark of fire that matched hers. Too late, she realized that its origin was different.

"What are you doing?" she whispered, her anger forgotten under his gentle headhold. All too near were the endless length of his body, the firm texture of his skin, the scent of aftershave. Her breath caught in her throat as he answered.

"Kissing you," he said, but he hesitated, his eyes touching each of her features in a sensuous visual foray. If he sought a sign of resistance, she was too stunned to offer it. Then, at last, he lowered his lips to catch her breath with a warm, strong kiss. It was undemanding yet enticing, exactly like the man himself.

Thrown by the sudden force of it all, Nia was numbed, momentarily robbed of the ability to respond. She could only stand before him and experience him in larger-than-life vividness. His mouth was rich as it sampled hers; his lips were firm and sure. The aura he cast was one of burgeoning masculinity, making a mockery of her temporarily blunted response. He was close and straight, seeming to draw her up to meet him. His hands held her face in up-tilted imprisonment; his fingers were gentle yet unyielding.

Beneath his tender persuasion she felt her stupor melting, giving way to a far greater force within, that of her own femininity. Whatever faults she could find with Daniel Strahan's affiliations and loyalties, he was the only man in years to reach this core.

With a small sigh of surrender she gave herself up to the headiness of him, savoring the increasing force of his kiss as he responded in turn to her awakening. His slanting lips were hungry, but hers were as eager to please. In the heat of excitement she opened mindlessly to him, welcoming the invasion of his tongue as it drove her responses higher. She was stunned now by a different force, that of desire, raw and overwhelming.

When Daniel dragged his lips from hers she felt the loss instantly. It was a throbbing disappointment to her newly roused senses, the withdrawal of a luxury she had enjoyed to the fullest. It had been no different for Daniel, if the unsteadiness of his breathing was proof. Holding her back, he looked down at her face, flushed, now, and warm. Then, as though sensing her emotion in its entirety, he brought her against him, into the fullness of his embrace for the very first time. It was a symbolic gesture; he had admitted her to his inner sanctum, had brought her past that wall of detachment that separated the inner man from the world. Nia sought the closeness without analysis, simply indulging in his strength. The sweetness of the moment was made more poignant by the tremor of his arms as his hold tightened. Then, with a final parting squeeze, he moved back.

It was Nia who first managed a shaky whisper. "What was *that* for?" Her violet eyes held a twinkle that spread quickly to sparkle beneath Daniel's roguishly arched brow.

"Hunger . . . ?" he drawled in innocent suggestiveness.

Slowly shaking her head, she laughed. "So we're back to that, are we?"

"Actually," he grew more serious, "you seem to have this way of stimulating it. Like sugar in the bloodstream. I've thought of you since yesterday."

"Not last night," she took quick exception. "Not during the game."

"Did you watch?"

Her look held a touch of guilt that instantly quelled his excitement. "I . . . almost . . ."

"What does *that* mean?"

"It means," she sighed, "that I couldn't quite get myself to turn on the set until it was too late." It was a small part of the story. How much easier it would have been to simply say she hadn't been home! But something in Daniel commanded the truth. Responding to his silent order, she further incriminated herself. "I . . . made it through the first couplet . . ."

"The first couplet?" he croaked uncertainly.

"You know, *'Oh, say, can you see . . .'* "

"Ahhh," he threw his head, facetiously mocking his own denseness, "*that* first couplet." Then, as understanding dawned, he frowned. "What you're saying is that you couldn't bring yourself to watch the game."

She shrugged in helpless admission, diverted her gaze, then skirted him to open the freezer. "Are you angry?" she asked, pushing aside several packages of vegetables to unearth the steak she had vetoed last night.

"No."

"You *could* be . . ." she goaded experimentally.

"No, Antonia." He took her arm and turned her around, shoving the freezer door back in place. "*I* couldn't be. You owe me nothing, certainly not a love for my game. Moreover," his dark brown eyes absorbed her attention, "knowing what little I do about you, I can begin to understand the way you feel. Rightly or wrongly, you associate the game of basketball with your past unhappiness. Although I'm sorry that that's the case, I can't begrudge you your honest feelings. Now," his face broke into an abrupt smile, lighting hers reflectively, "I *would* have been angry had you told me you weren't home last night. . . ."

A smile found its way to her lips. Thank goodness, she mused, recalling her thoughts of earlier. The coincidence of hearing him echo them blinded her to a possible second meaning in his vow. "I *was* home. And I do know that you won. Congratulations."

With a shrug, he released her. "Where *is* that corkscrew?"

But if Nia thought that the matter of her conditioned response to basketball was to be dropped, she was mistaken. For no sooner had Daniel uncorked the wine and filled the glasses she handed him than he leaned back against the counter, crossed his ankles, and stared thoughtfully ahead. Nia put a wad of butter in the frying pan to melt, then set to slicing onions.

"Were you ever a basketball fan?" he asked softly, nonbelligerently.

"No." The first onion's papery sheath slid off with a crackle into her hand.

"You disliked the game from the start?"

"No. I, uh, I never really got to know it." The heavy knife cleanly cut one slice, then another.

"David didn't talk to you about it?"

"I overheard him talking to other people, but he never discussed it all that much with me." A third, fourth and fifth slice fell onto the cutting board. Crinkling her nose against the smell, Nia reached for another onion.

"How could that be? You were married for five years. If basketball was as much a part of him as I assume, what was there left to talk about?"

The parched skin crinkled loudly. "There *is* more to life than—"

"I know." He apologized, instantly aware of her tension and intent on alleviating it. "That came out wrong. I'm just wondering how you avoided learning about something that was such a vital part of him."

With several slices cut from the second onion, the smell had grown stronger. "David and I talked of other things. Our relationship was a novelty to us. In many ways, the attraction was as irresponsible as it was immature. I suppose I was as drawn to David's age as he was to my lack of it. At first. Then . . . well . . ." Eyes tearing, she sniffled.

Daniel's fingers circled her wrist in a gentle bid for attention. "I'm sorry, Nia. I didn't mean to upset you. If thinking of him makes you cry, I won't mention it again."

"It's the onions!" she protested, lifting her free hand to dab at the moisture in her eyes. "I may still feel the pain of my marriage, but I stopped shedding tears for it long ago." When he released her wrist she reached for the last onion. "Why are you harping on this, anyway?"

"Just curious."

"About David?" She hid her expression as she sliced away.

"No, Antonia," he drawled in good-natured punishment. "About *you.* I'm trying to understand you."

"Oh, God, this is horrible!" she cried with a loud sniffle. "I can't see what I'm doing through these damned tears!"

"Here, let me finish."

Half wondering if he could, Nia turned the knife over to him while she sought refuge at the distant end of the kitchen, as far as possible from the odorous storm center. Her eyes had barely dried when a tell-tale sizzle from the pan verified Daniel's accomplishment.

"Thanks." She ventured back into the fray, taking the wine glass he offered. "Say, you did that very well. I thought you said you didn't cook."

The spark of warm chocolate in his gaze tickled

her deep inside. "I said that I'm not a very *good* cook. I can do the little chores, like slicing onions, but I need someone like you to direct the action."

Emboldened by the gentle intimacy of sharing, Nia took the bull by the horns. It was about time she learned something about Daniel. Best to start with his avowed strengths, then slyly move on. "I understand that you're fully in charge of your team. Ten straight is terrific!"

The swirl of red liquid in his glass caught his eye. "I hate to tally them up like that. It's far safer to take it one game at a time."

"Surely you have to be *encouraged* by a winning streak. . . ."

"It could turn at any time."

"Are you always a pessimist?"

"I'm always a realist."

"But Chris tells me that the whole season has been great. How can you help but look ahead to the playoffs?"

"Who's Chris?"

If that was jealousy, it was a boost to her feminine ego. "He's a senior editor at *Eastern Edge.* He adores the Breakers. He thinks that *you're* . . . brilliant was the exact word he used."

"That's nice." Lifting the glass to his lips, he sipped its contents slowly.

"Aren't you pleased?"

"Uh-huh."

"Daniel," she straightened, clearly confused, "I don't quite understand you. Your team is on a hot streak, your own fans rave about you, and you don't even crack a smile?"

He did crack a smile for her just then, but it held a trace of sadness. "It's only a game, Nia. The winning, the fame, the glory—it's all fleeting. The public is fickle. They'd as soon boo you off the court if you miss six running as cheer. It's not all glamour, as most people think. There's a negative side to it as well."

Nia had only to glance at the fast sautéing onions for Daniel to take the long-handled wooden spoon and stir them. "Tell me about it," she urged him softly. "That negative side."

Long moments passed before he spoke, moments during which he organized his thoughts. "The traveling is tough; I've mentioned that to you before. The road trips consist of one flight after another, odd mealtimes, strange hotel rooms, unfamiliar locker rooms. Then there's the precarious status of the players themselves. All it takes is one injury for the entire makeup of a team to change."

"Are they common?"

"Injuries? Very. Take the Breakers. We've played our last six games without benefit of our starting center and a forward. Walker took an elbow in the face that required plastic surgery; Barnes hit the floor the wrong way and wrenched his knee. They were two of our key players, lost with the hottest part of the season just beginning. Philadelphia is only five games out; we can't afford to lose many."

Nia got a glimpse of worry lines on Daniel's brow. She'd never seen them before. If talking out the problem would help ease them, she'd talk readily. "What did you do—about Walker and Barnes?"

"There's not much I can do. They'll be out for several more games apiece. What I have done is re-organize the offense. It's working out well." He looked up more hopefully. "I've brought Rockowski in as back-up center. He's a bruiser, can hold his own and pass it around. Flagg is also on the court longer, with Barnes out. He's young, but his game matures with each outing." Pausing, he chuckled softly, then shook his head.

Nia smiled. "What is it?"

"They call him 'Sandman'—Johnny Flagg. He's super laid-back and relaxed. Sleeps just about anywhere. *Everywhere.*"

Her gaze grew suspicious. "And what do they call 'the bruiser'?"

Daniel's smile was a broad one. "Rocky . . ."

"That's what I thought." She turned to unwrap the steak and flip on the broiler before unveiling the surf side of the impromptu feast.

"Lobster?" Daniel's eyes lit up. "Boy, you literary types sure know how to feed a guy."

"This was *my* lobster, I'll have you know. I shopped for it in the rain, no less, as a special treat."

"Hard day at work?"

With a grimace, she recalled a major source of her frustration. He stood right beside her now. "Fair."

"What are you working on?"

"Oh, no, Daniel Strahan. You haven't finished what *you* were saying."

"What *was* I saying?" He reached to help Nia remove the broiler pan from the upper oven. As she lined it with foil, he glanced around. "Would you like me to make a salad?"

"A salad? Think you're up to it?"

"I make a *good* salad," he scolded playfully.

She grinned. "Then, go to it." She presented him with a large bowl. "Everything you'll need is in there," she informed him, pointing to the refrigerator before turning to slice the thick lobster tails.

"Have you lived here long?" he asked, his voice muffled behind the refrigerator door. She could just imagine his wise grin and it made her that much more determined not to be sidetracked.

"What else bothers you?" she asked firmly.

"Bothers me?"

"About . . . your job."

"Oh." He paused. "I thought it made you uncomfortable to talk about basketball."

"It does, in a way. But that all had to do with David. Now I'm curious about you. I've told you all about my marriage; the least you can do is to tell me about your work."

Nia was unprepared for his darkening. "Is this for the record?"

"You mean, for the piece I've got to write?"

He dipped his head in the affirmative. Before her very eyes, she saw the mask begin to descend.

"No, this is *not* for the record. In the first place, you haven't agreed to my interview. In the second place, I don't want to do the damn thing, anyway!"

The mask receded. "Whew. That's that, I guess," he mocked her vehemence. "Well, then, what do you want to know?"

"Those other frustrations. What are they?"

Daniel spoke as he emptied her refrigerator of every possible salad fixing. "I've already mentioned the traveling and the injuries. Then there are the fans. Not only can they be fickle, but they can be downright demoralizing."

"How so?" she asked, puzzled. "I would think they'd just roll off your backs."

"Let me tell you, ma'am—when a twelve-year-old kid looks you in the eye from his seat overlooking the tunnel and tells you what a so-and-so you were for not beating the such-and-such out of your opponent, it's demoralizing. Or when you're in the middle of the fourth quarter and the back-up you put in blows one shot after the next—and the fan in the tenth row announces that you were an absolute imbecile for putting the guy in in the first place. Little things like that."

"I'm sure you must get used to some of it."

"You turn it off, yes. But it does have a way of sneaking through every once in a while. When the team's winning you can thumb your nose at just about any fan. When you lose, even if it's only by a point, then it's not as easy. That's why I try to take it *all* with a grain of salt. I do my best as a coach; beyond that, nothing is certain."

"Even your job?"

"Especially my job."

"But . . . don't you have a contract?"

There was a cynical edge to his laugh, punctuated by the steady slicing of carrots. "Contracts can be crumpled and burned at any time."

"That's awful," she exclaimed, shaken by the instability of the picture he'd painted. "Doesn't that bother you? Doesn't it affect your coaching ability?"

He deftly lifted the cutting board and scraped carrots, green peppers and radishes into the salad bowl. "As I told you before, I'm realistic. I keep things in perspective. Despite what *you* may believe, there *is* more to life than basketball."

"Oh, *I* believe it," she countered quickly, cocking a skeptical eye his way. "I'm just surprised to hear that *you* do."

"Don't ever judge a book by its cover, Nia," he drawled, seizing the head of iceberg lettuce and tossing it high into the air before slamming it flat onto the counter. With a confident twist he turned it over and wrenched off the heel that the blow had dislodged. Then, calmly, nonchalantly, he put the entire head beneath the cold water faucet.

Nia had followed the maneuver wide-eyed. "*That* was quite a show," she laughed. "Now, if you had dribbled it around, I might have worried. . . ."

"No cause. Didn't I tell you I made a good salad?"

"Hmmm," was the only response she could muster. This was *not* the Daniel Strahan she had expected to find. With the little he was slowly divulging, she found herself more and more curious. Unfortunately, between setting the table in the dining room and broiling the sirloin to the proper rareness, serious conversation was left hanging until they sat, at last, across from one another at the bleached elm table. Looking down at her plate, Nia couldn't restrain herself. "This is what you'd call a mixed bag."

"Some bag! I'll take half-steak, half-lobster any day!"

"You're willing to foot that kind of bill?"

"If . . ." he lowered his voice, "I had someone to share it with. This is lovely, Antonia." Their eyes met and held, then parted.

"It *is* nice," she mused softly, reflecting on the pleasantness of companionship once in a while. *Once in a while*—that's all she'd get with a man like this. He would be off and running before long. "So, what's on tap for the team? Are you off to God-knows-where next week?"

"We are. It's a short trip, though. New York, New Jersey and finally Pennsylvania."

"Pennsylvania!" she exclaimed. *"I'll* be there next week, too."

"You will?"

"Yes. I'm doing a feature story on the Amish. I'll be spending two days driving around the country-side between Reading and Lancaster."

"Are you driving down from here?"

"Uh-uh. That would take too long. I'd planned to fly into Philadelphia and rent a car from there. It's just a matter of making the final reservations."

He nodded. "I see. . . . You're going alone?"

"Looks that way. The man with the money is generous when it comes to travel allowances, but he's not about to throw it away on an unnecessary entourage." She lifted her fork. "Actually, I prefer it that way."

"Traveling alone?"

"Yes. I can really *work;* then, as soon as I've got

what I need, I come home." That was the advantage of traveling alone, but there were disadvantages, too, such as the lack of a familiar face in a strange place, or, more simply stated, loneliness.

"Do you travel often?"

"On and off. This is an 'on' period. I'm even hoping to get out to the West Coast on an assignment."

"The West Coast? For *Eastern Edge?*"

With a patient smile she told him of the sister publication for which she was hoping to write a contributing article. "My family lives in San Francisco."

"Really! Is that where you grew up?"

"Uh-huh. My parents and brothers still live there. I also have a married sister in Seattle. I'm the one who really broke from the mold." Her features tensed in recollection of the sharp differences of opinion she'd had with her parents.

"When you married?"

"Before that. Long before that." She grinned guiltily, then explained. "I was rebellious as a teenager—never could seem to learn when not to argue. In spite of myself, I did well in school and on my college boards, though. I was accepted at Stanford and Radcliffe. When I decided to come east, my parents were not thrilled." She gave added emphasis to the last two words. "Then, David and I eloped . . . against their wishes. They temporarily disowned me."

"Temporarily?"

"Mmmm," she agreed, savoring a bite of sautéd lobster meat. "I guess it's true that blood runs thicker than water. In time they came around. They had almost begun to accept the marriage when it fell apart."

Having ravished his lobster first, Daniel raised his knife to cut his steak, then paused. "How did they react to that?"

Nia's shoulders lifted in a sigh of appreciation, of genuine respect. "What can I say? They were wonderful. I had expected a never-ending stream of I-told-you-so's. There wasn't *one.* I was pretty shaken and they seemed to understand that. My mother even flew out to stay here for a week. We got to know each other . . . as adults. It was very nice."

"Do you go back there often?"

"Once or twice a year. I flew back last November for Thanksgiving. If I can wrangle this *Western Edge* assignment, I may get there again next month."

"Next month?" he asked, eyeing her more alertly. "You *do* get around."

For a few minutes they ate in silence, lost in their own thoughts. Nia's were surprisingly relaxed, centered on the pleasantness of Daniel's company. It was only when curiosity got the better of her again that she spoke.

"If this was an 'off' day, what have you been doing? What *does* a coach do when there is no game?" It was one of the very questions she'd asked herself the night before, after the game she hadn't had the courage to watch. With Daniel here and in a seemingly receptive mood, she had nothing to lose by asking . . . particularly when she had just gone on about herself at *his* bidding.

At first he remained silent, eyes downcast, fork poised above his plate. Was he hesitant about speaking, even after that embrace and the opening she thought she'd sensed? Had she imagined that . . . or simply wished it?

The mellowing of his features spoke of a decision reached in her favor. His smile curled its way right down to her toes. "I love the way people assume that a 'free' day is *totally* 'free.' For the players it means a two-or three-hour practice, perhaps a team meeting, a movie. For me it means work on top of that—management meetings, films—"

"Films? A movie? Where does Hollywood fit into the sport?"

Daniel laughed. "I'm not talking about the standard Saturday night fare, though there's many a Saturday night I do watch them. No, these movies are of the homemade variety, films of the team we'll be playing next, even films of our last game with that team. It helps to understand the strengths and strategies of the opposition in planning our offense."

Nia nodded her understanding. "So where does the coach fit into these practices and meetings and showings?"

"I *run* it all. I direct the practice, conduct the meetings, give a running commentary on the film as it rolls. For each time the team sees a film, I've seen it twice."

"Really? But why?"

"In order for me to effectively coach, I need to know both the opposition *and* my own players like the back of my hand. I need to know how each one reacts in certain situations, against certain types of players." His eyes glowed with inner satisfaction. "To my way of thinking, my greatest challenge as a coach is in the understanding, the behind-the-scenes study that results in the correct anticipation of a successful play." Realizing that he'd divulged a little bit of himself, he hesitated, then grinned to lighten the air. "And besides, Harlan loves the movies. And he doesn't like to watch alone. He prefers to have three or four of us in there with him."

She frowned, not immediately placing the name. "Harlan . . . ?"

"McKay. President and General Manager of the team."

"Harlan McKay . . ." she repeated the name softly. "Harlan McKay . . . of course."

"You knew him?"

"David knew him. And well, I think. I've never met the man."

Having finished eating, Daniel sat back in his chair, leaving one long arm and its strong-fingered hand on the table. "Harlan is . . . an experience." The twinkle in his eye spoke of a certain fondness. "He's roughly sixty years of age, a widower who lives alone and has made the New England Breakers his family."

"Is he easy to work for?"

"Easy?" He rolled the word around his tongue as though trying to taste its meaning. "Easy is a relative term. I find him easy to live with because I'm confident in what I do and therefore unthreatened by his peculiarities. I have, however, lost two assistant coaches because of him, and I've had to deal with the ruffled feathers of many of my players in the four years since I've been coach." He smiled with an air of that very confidence of which he'd spoken instants before. "I think I've finally got Harlan under control, though."

Nia's eyes widened. "What, exactly, does the man do that irritates everyone?"

Daniel chuckled. "He lives the game twenty-four hours a day. I mean, when I tell you that he's often called me at six in the morning to discuss a particular play he wants considered . . ."

"Oh, no . . ."

"Oh, yes! He broods constantly, analyzes every second of playing time, second-guesses everyone and everything. It can, on occasion, be troublesome."

"I can believe it! But, how do *you* deal with him?"

"I anticipate his needs and try to satisfy them in a way that's compatible with *my* life."

"By winning?" she asked.

"By understanding Harlan. I think that he's basically a very lonely gentleman who has no one to discuss his fears with. He desperately wants the franchise to be a successful one, and he worries constantly. Don't get me wrong—he's a genius at scouting out fresh talent and then securing it for us. He understands the business end of the sport; under his management, the Breakers have turned in record high profits. But he is . . . a pest. If I'm willing to hold his hand every so often, he's content. So I simply pick my time and place for these booster sessions. By prearranging a meeting with him in his office this morning, for example, I tempered his impulse to call at dawn." Pausing, he took a concluding breath. "Anyway, I think I've finally convinced him that I can do the job."

"My Lord, with the Breakers' record, he should be convinced!"

"Touché." Daniel smiled with quiet modesty.

"But tell me, Daniel, what is it that you *like* about your job?" she prodded softly. "You've mentioned lots of minus points. What are the plusses?"

His response held no hesitancy. "The game," he stated with a gently helpless smile. "I love the game. I always have. I always will. When I was a kid—" he began, then cut himself off just as Nia perked up. It would have been the first time he'd talked of his childhood. Her disappointment was eased, however, by the positively endearing look of excitement that brought his features alive.

"Ach, it's still the same! There's that very special feeling when the rhythm is right, just right." His hand made a flowing motion, simulating a gently undulating wave. "You know it's there. Everything comes together." He spoke more softly, with the drama of reenactment. "You take the ball on the rebound and make a fast break, hurl an outlet pass downcourt, then follow while your teammates pass it on the outside. You slice in through the center, outstretch your opponent's attempted block to snatch the ball from high in the air . . . then you hook it through the hoop in one continuous motion." Nia listened to every word, entranced by the boyish enthusiasm and very evident devotion that emerged. "Whew!" He shook his head in amazement, as though he had just physically executed the play and couldn't quite believe it. "It's great!"

In the wake of his impassioned replay Nia could only smile and accept the fact that Daniel Strahan did, indeed, love his game. He had spent far less actual time on this brief discourse than he had spent on the negative aspects of his work, yet his enthrallment with it was indisputable.

"Sorry." He grimaced in belated embarrassment. "I get carried away every once in a while. I didn't mean to bore you."

"Bore me? That was great!" It had been impossible not to catch his excitement.

His gaze sharpened. "It didn't upset you?"

"You mean . . . because of David?" At Daniel's nod she tried to explain, to herself as well as to him. "It's somehow different . . . when you speak of it. I can see now why you put up with the strange hotel rooms and the phone calls at six, not to mention your goons yelling 'Heeey, Professor' . . ." She caught her breath. "Why *did* he call you that?"

He shrugged off the significance of the nickname. "I got tagged that way when I was a player. You know these media people." He lowered his voice pointedly. "They love tossing around nicknames. Makes them feel knowledgeable. The joke in the league is that a rookie knows he's made it when a nickname sticks. *Our* rookie made it this year."

"Oh?" She met his expectant grin with one of her own. "Do tell."

Eagerly, he launched into an explanation. "Luke Walker. From Indiana State. His specialty is the sky hook. They call him . . . 'Skyman.' "

Resting her elbow on the table, Nia propped a hand beneath her chin. "Luke 'Skyman' Walker? You can't be serious . . ." His nod refuted her claim. "That's too much. But . . . what about 'Professor'? How did you come by that particular tag?"

Daniel's gaze beamed straight into her. If she thought to trick him into divulging personal information under the umbrella of basketball, she was mistaken. Having decided on his own that the time was right, he spoke carefully, quite conscious of each word.

"I've always been a reader—on the plane, waiting for buses, whiling away the idle hours. On the road I often escape to a local library. It's one way of being with old friends."

She could understand exactly; she viewed bookstores in much the same light. "I know the feeling. But . . . there has to be more behind the moniker. . . ."

He hesitated before continuing. "There is. I take courses at Harvard whenever I can fit them into my schedule. I'm often caught studying for exams."

Nia's face brightened at the image he'd created. "You are? That's great! What do you study?" She was fascinated. It was certainly a new twist to the stereotypical career athlete.

Having come this far, Daniel took a breath. Slowly, he let it out. "Psychology. Human behavior." He watched her reaction closely. "I'm interested in what makes people do what they do."

Nia couldn't suppress the grin that slid to her warm lips. "So *that's* why you've asked me so many questions about my background . . . and about my relationship with David. You're analyzing me!" There was a note of accusation in her voice, but it was mild and without real condemnation.

"No, Antonia." He softly caressed her name as his eyes echoed the action. "I'm only trying to understand you."

She heard his words, yet it was what he hadn't said that troubled her. Why did he wish to understand her? What was it he wanted? Did he see her as friend or foe, woman or writer? Was he struggling with the distinction just as she was?

As confusion clouded her gaze his grew more taut as well, as though to confirm her final thought. Despite the ease that had characterized the conversation during dinner, neither could come to broach this particularly personal vein. For Nia's part, she wasn't sure what to say. For Dan's, he was still wary of saying it.

The awkward silence was broken when he cleared his throat. "Here. Let me give you a hand with these dishes," he offered, pushing back his chair and standing to tower above the table.

Motivated by nervous energy, Nia wasn't far behind. "No, no. That's all right. I'll take care of them later." Intuitively, she knew she'd need that scrubbing time to work Daniel out of her system once he'd left. But he ignored her and proceeded to carefully stack the plates, then headed for the kitchen. "Daniel . . . please!" she protested. "There's really no need."

Putting the flatwear on the counter, he determinedly shoved up the sleeves of his sweater and rolled his shirt cuffs back. "I'll just do the broiler pan," he growled. "You can take care of the rest later."

Had her voice been working properly, Nia would have verbally acquiesced. But something in her throat discouraged sound, a something relating to the sight of two forearms, sinewed and straight, brushed with a most masculine helping of dark brown hair. Daniel reached to turn on the water. Her eyes followed his hand, then worked back over his wrist to the strength she so admired. What woman in her right mind would not want that hand stroking her or that arm crushing her against the granite wall of an equally well-muscled chest?

Those arms—warm, manly, strong. She drew in a swift breath at the reckless rush of sensation brought by the sight of those arms—his arms. Whirling, she escaped to the living room.

There she sat, ensconced in a cushioned corner of the sofa, legs curled up beneath her, thinking of Daniel Strahan. How could he excite her so? What was the nature of the power he wielded to render her so utterly malleable before him? Even now, in hindsight, the thought of that warm, naked skin gave her goose bumps, which in turn sent ripples of awareness through her whole body. He was handsome and appealing . . . and he excited her! It was pleasant and terrifying; how could she reconcile the two?

Head bowed in study of the ivory lengths of her

fingers, she felt a warmth on her neck even before his hand curved gently at its nape.

"Are you all right, Nia?" he asked softly, propping his other hand on the sofa back and leaning in toward her. Had *he* scrubbed out the demons of desire on the charred grate of her broiler pan?

She nodded, silently praying that he would exercise good sense for them both and withdraw his hand. She simply couldn't ask it. But his fingers began to move then, slowly massaging the tension from her neck in long, sensuous strokes, replacing it with a tingling that slithered through the curves of her body. Closing her eyes, she heard a soft cry, a vocal aching, and only realized she'd made it when Daniel leaned closer.

"Nia?"

She opened her eyes and stared at him, unable to mask the birth of desire sparked by his return. His forearms were still bare; she craved to touch them but didn't quite dare. Daniel read her frustration and came slowly to sit beside her. His eyes were molten brown probes touching her cheek, her nose, her soft, moist lips. Nia sensed the hammering of her heart as his gaze dropped lower to the firm swell of her breasts. He could have stripped her naked; she felt the heat surging through her intensifying.

Her name this time was almost a moan on his lips as he accepted her silent invitation and kissed her, lacing the long fingers of one hand through her hair, wrapping the other arm behind her. And Nia went to him willingly, for protest at this stage was impossible. The surface innocence of the evening's conversation had held a subtle intimacy, one that had combined with chemical attraction to inspire precisely this.

Daniel worshipped her lips, then her eyes, cheeks and neck in turn. At each stop he brewed up delicious feelings that she relished to the deepest core of her womanhood. She gave him blind access to whatever he wished, craving only the continuation of this raw delight. It was a fitting dessert to the spontaneous dinner they'd shared. She'd take his embrace over a hot fudge sundae anytime!

If his own crescendoing ardor lent an edge of fierceness to his kiss, Nia was unaware of the change, for it paralleled her own state of heightened desire. Returning everything he gave, she abandoned herself to the joy of a physical intimacy that threatened to wipe all other thoughts from her mind.

But Daniel's sudden shudder prevented that. Tearing his lips away, moving them to her ear, then up to her rich mahogany crown, he rasped hoarsely, "God, Nia! This is wrong! I know it is. You deserve something steady—something I can't give you." He looked down into her eyes, shocking her with the dark intensity of his expression. "But I can't stay away. I can't just . . . let it go. Do you understand what I'm trying to say?"

Nia was held spellbound by his fervent gaze, just as she was held firmly within the reassuring band of his arms. She had seen such earnestness in him only once—earlier, when he had spoken of his love for basketball. Was she forever to compete with that game for the attentions of a man?

Yet she could muster no anger as she admired his features, for they were strong and welcoming, bidding her to fight for what she wanted. Touching each of those features, one by one, with her own violet gaze, she finally forced a whisper. "I wish I could understand all of this—*any* of this. But I don't. I only know what I feel at one given moment . . ." At this given moment, she wanted to touch him.

Slowly lifting her hand to his face, she traced each commanding feature in turn, then dared to let her fingers trail down the broad column of his neck to the place where his shirt collar lay open. That place, that vee, had tantalized her all evening. Now she yielded to temptation and, at last, knew the feel of his manly skin beneath her fingertips. It was hot and textured, throbbing as she slid her fingers beneath shirt and sweater to rest more closely against his collarbone.

This was a new and heady landscape to be explored, and she had only just begun. On impulse, she stretched to put her lips where her fingers had been, kissing his skin gently.

"You smell so good," she murmured, breathing in his musk-scented masculinity.

As he took her chin, Daniel's hand shook slightly. But he, too, knew what he wanted at that instant. Turning her face up, he renewed his kiss, coaxing her tongue to join his in play. This time it was his hand that traced her neck to her throat, but it didn't stop at the fabric of her top. Rather, it moved more tentatively to her chest, slowly, gently circling one breast, then the other. He sensed her reflexive arching and cupped her fullness with more confidence as she cried her pleasure aloud.

"Oh, Daniel. Do you have any idea what you do to me?"

"Tell me, Nia," he commanded raggedly, as deeply affected by his giving as she was by the receiving of it.

"You've set me afire," she whispered. "It keeps spreading and spreading, deep inside where I can't quench the flame."

"That's good, babe," he crooned as he passed his palms across her breasts, feeling their pebbled reflex even through her clothing. With a small cry, Nia opened her lips to his descent, needing more, always more.

Daniel Strahan had ceased to be simply a bug in her ear. With the awesome scope of this physicality that drew her inexorably closer to him, he was no less than a source of sustenance, suddenly crucial to her survival.

Her hands were restless in their exploration of the solidity of his shoulders as she arched at his touch, wanting to know everything about this man, every intimate thing. The fact that he had once been a basketball star seemed relevant only in his skillful handling of her body. In this he was as masterful as any man she'd ever known; he was truly outstanding. He knew when to tease or rub, when to skim or press, when to knead or circle. His lovemaking had a rhythm to it that was just right, that simply flowed.

Nia flowed with it, threading her fingers through the vibrancy of his hair to hold him close as his tongue swept into her mouth. In a deft shift, he drew her around and put her gently down on her back on the sofa.

Then his hands and lips caressed her with even greater freedom, sending her on vibrant bursting waves of rapture. She sighed her pleasure when his hands found the ribbed band of her sweater and pushed it up, past her midriff and then further, over the enticing, tautly crested peaks of her breasts.

For a minute he looked down at her, adoring her flesh with eyes that smoldered. The sight of her cream-skinned breasts clothed only in the delicate lace of her bra sent a visible tremor through his limbs.

"How lovely you are," he whispered as he lifted a finger to touch one nipple. The contact was a searing one; Nia sharply bit her lip to keep from crying out.

"Daniel . . ." She reached for him, drawing him down to kiss her again. But his lips were impatient, leaving hers after a short, bold kiss, lowering to taste the compelling warmth of her breast. "Mmmmm . . . Daniel . . ." she cried, writhing beneath him, straining upward as he drew back her bra's lacy cup and took the fullness of her nipple and its surrounding rosy skirt into his mouth. His leisurely sucking nearly drove her to distraction, as it fanned her fire into a white-hot flame of desire. When his hand fell to her knee and moved upward, over her denim-sheathed thigh, then dangerously inland, conflagration seemed imminent.

Suddenly they had reached the bottom line, the end goal of this passion-play. With shock, Nia realized that she wanted Daniel to make love to her. Without a thought for his job or hers, his history or hers, the propriety of any of it—she wanted his total possession. Nothing less would satisfy the deep ache of tension that had gathered and built within her.

The awareness of what had to follow came to Daniel simultaneously. As he raised his head to meet her wide-eyed gaze her hand fell from the thickness of his hair to his broad shoulders, then to the upper arms whose brawn could easily sustain him over her . . . should they go with the flow of passion.

But he was the coach, calling the plays. With trembling hands and a regretful cast of his fathomless brown eyes, he eased her sweater back over her breasts and further down to her waist. If Nia felt the loss of his touch she had only to listen to the ragged scratch of his voice to imagine what his restraint had cost him.

"I'm sorry, Nia. I can't do this to you." A cold trickle of apprehension worked its way around her insides. What was he saying? And why that self-righteous note? "Much as I want you, it wouldn't be good for either of us. You're the media—I'm into basketball. You hate basketball—I distrust the media. It would never work."

Her own perplexity held her motionless. *What* would never work? she wondered—one night in bed . . . or more? He had singled out the one point that had to be considered. What puzzled her was why he had done so before taking his pleasure with her. His arousal had been clear; he had just admitted his desire. Why had he stopped? On principle alone?

They had been playing on Nia's home court, but suddenly the initiative was stolen from them. With ten times the force of the referee's whistle the blast of a car horn shattered the night, its continued blare boding ill for its driver.

Daniel stiffened. "What in the devil is *that?* Do you have teenagers around?"

As he shifted to allow her passage, Nia bolted up. All thought of passion vanished beneath a sweep of personal concern and proprietorial responsibility. "My God, it must be Dr. Max . . . !"

five

NIA RACED TO THE DOOR, LEAVING IT AJAR as she tore downstairs and outside, Daniel close on her heels. When they retraced their steps at a more leisurely pace several moments later, they were purged of carnal cravings.

"Does he do that often?" Daniel asked. His amusement tempered the air as he crossed the living room to retrieve the trenchcoat he'd dropped there earlier.

He intended to leave, and although Nia believed it to be for the best, she still had mixed feelings. In a nonchalant gesture she tossed her head back to dislodge any moistness lingering from the pale drizzle outside. The chill that touched her was only partly due to that cold night air; the rest was in anticipation of the soul-searching she knew lay ahead.

"He's never done *that* before!" she exclaimed with affection. "There have been any number of other quirks—lights left on, phone fallen off the hook, kitchen timer ringing for hours, outgoing mail, even bills dropped on the driveway—but never," her eyes registered belated humor, "a book carton jammed against the steering wheel."

"Against the horn," Daniel corrected, grinning. "Well, if nothing else, it was guaranteed to get help . . . and quickly."

In response to his meaningful gaze, Nia lowered her eyes. She, too, recalled what Dr. Max's mini-calamity had interrupted. "Thanks for giving him a hand, Dan," she murmured self-consciously. "It just didn't occur to him to walk around the car and take the carton out from the passenger's side. It was good of you to carry it in for him."

Daniel scoffed off any effort. "It was nothing."

"He's such a sweet man . . . and he does try so hard to function on his own."

"Is he alone? Does he have family nearby?"

"Oh, yes. He has a daughter living in Belmont, only ten minutes from here. But he refuses to move. He claims he'd be in the way of her husband and the kids. But the kids are in college and there's a perfect little suite he could have, off at an end of the house and on his own. But he's a stubborn one." She shrugged. "Crotchety in his old age, I guess."

Daniel chuckled sadly. "I know the type."

Something in his tone brought her quickly alert. It was a quiet, faraway quality, suggesting that his knowledge stemmed from personal experience. But before Nia could find the words to ask him about it, he had put on his coat.

"Thanks for dinner, Nia." He smiled gently. "It was a nice change."

"Home-cooked?" she teased, fighting her disappointment.

"Yes." He stood about an arm's reach—an easy arm's reach, given the length of his limbs—from her, yet made no move to close the distance. Though there was no sign of the intense desire she had seen earlier, his expression bore a gratifying warmth. Slowly it spread through her, bringing with it a return of the comfortable feeling she had known for so much of the evening. She liked Daniel Strahan.

"You're sure I can't tempt you with coffee?" she asked softly.

His dark head shook slowly from side to side, his eyes holding hers, his lips twitching at the corners. "Poor choice of words, babe. You tempt me far too much as it is."

"The offer was made in good faith," she chided, refusing to blush at the innuendo.

"Thanks . . . but no. I've got to get home to watch a game."

Nia couldn't help but grimace. "I might've known." She feigned dismay, then frowned in puzzlement. "A game? At this hour?"

"Actually, it's a rerun of the game we played last night. I have one of those machines on my set—"

"A video recorder?"

"Right. It's very handy. If I set it on a timer, it tapes the game. I can rerun it at my own convenience, in the comfort—as they say in the ads—of my own home."

"Where's that?" she asked, eyes innocently rounded. She had been hoping to take advantage of his relaxed smile, but he was too quick to turn over any information by accident.

He eyed her knowingly, with an air of smugness. "Not far from the arena." He was purposely vague. "There are several portions of the game I've got to study." His features grew more pensive. "I'm not sure about the effectiveness of several of our moves. And I've got to decide before practice tomorrow whether to go with them again or chuck them."

Nia conceded defeat gracefully. "Is there a game tomorrow?"

"We're playing Houston."

"Tough game?"

"Every game's tough."

"Think you can win?"

"That's why we play."

Nia shot him a look of mock astonishment. "I was wondering about that . . ."

Daniel stepped closer in playful warning. "Smart. . . . Will you watch?" It came on her so quickly that she was unprepared.

"Watch?"

"The game."

"It's going to be televised?" she asked in a bid for time, as she groped for an answer.

"You know it is," he growled. "Will you watch?"

She nodded too quickly. "I'll try."

His voice dropped, weighed down by skepticism. "I'll . . . bet . . ."

"I *will* . . . try."

He narrowed one eye. "Really?"

"Uh-huh."

All playfulness seemed to suddenly fall away. "I'd like that," he stated with such soft sincerity that she almost believed it *might* mean something to him. Once more she was thrown into a web of confusion woven loosely around her alternatives. What did *she* want to do? But again Daniel called the shots. In this case, it was the final play of the night.

Lifting his hand to her neck, he curved his fingers around to her nape and let the firm pad of his thumb trace the softness of her lips. "Thanks, again," he murmured, then was gone.

Reeling in the wake of the abrupt shift from sensuality to departure, Nia voiced the first thought she could find in her muddled brain. "What about my article?" she called down the stairs at his fast-descending back.

"I'll give you a call," was his parting shout, instants before the front door slammed behind him.

Bewildered, Nia stared at the empty hallway. "You'll give me a call," she murmured. "That's just great. And what am I supposed to do in the meantime? Damn it, I'm right back to square one!"

But she wasn't. Not by a long shot. As she lay in her bed that night it seemed infinitely lonely. Her thoughts were filled with sweet memories, visions of long arms and seductively strong fingers, touching and caressing, stoking fires that had been banked for years.

It was only in theory that the *Eastern Edge* feature remained up in the air. Nia knew, without a doubt, that she would never use Daniel as one of the five eligible easterners Bill had chosen for her half of the story. She had known it from the start. Was there, then, any point to the pretense that she would? Shouldn't she simply tell Daniel she'd dropped the idea? Shouldn't she simply announce her failure to Bill and let him take the steps necessary in finding a replacement? Let Bill talk to Daniel if he wanted to test the coach's determination! At the very thought, she laughed. Daniel Strahan would no more grant that interview to Bill Austen than she would sit through a Breakers' game. . . . Or would she?

"Chris! I've been looking all over for you!"

"Hi, Nia!" Sandy hair tousled, cheeks unusually ruddy, Christopher Daly had just blown in from the windy plains of State Street. "Sorry about that. I had an errand to run down by the waterfront. Uh . . . have you got a special problem?"

They came together from opposite ends of the corridor, meeting by the doorway to Chris' office. Nia cut a properly sophisticated figure in her fitted suit of soft blue tweed. Chris was far more irreverent in an elbow-patched blazer and jeans. Mercifully, Bruce McHale was liberal on that score.

"Ah," she gave him a good-natured once-over, "so this is a sexy professor day?"

"Now, now," her friend drew himself up and hooked his thumbs in his back pockets, "can I help it if I understand comfort?"

"Anything new with Tricia?" Nia asked, changing the subject and whispering conspiratorially.

"Jennifer," he murmured with a smug smile.

"Tricia is seeing Jennifer?"

"*I'm* seeing Jennifer." He thumped his chest for emphasis.

"What about Tricia?"

His sheepish shrug said it all.

"Over?" Nia asked, ever-astonished at the turnover. For a thirty-seven-year-old bachelor, Chris Daly showed no signs of slowing down.

"Guess so. But you'd like Jennifer, Nia. She's a sweetheart—a psychologist. Great to talk to!"

"Is she?" Funny he should make the connection. Daniel's interest was also psychology, and he, too, was great to talk to. Perhaps it went with the field . . . which brought Nia to her immediate concern. "Listen, Chris, can you do me a favor?"

With a paternal arm about her shoulders, Chris ushered her into his office. The slot of senior editor carried with it its own private space. Though similar in decor to the room shared by Nia and Priscilla, Chris' was less than neat.

"Name it," he ordered, granting her a gallant carte-blanche.

She did. Without hesitancy. "Daniel Strahan. I want to know everything *you* do about the man."

"You're going forward on that assignment?"

"Yes." It wasn't a total lie. She was meeting that afternoon with Wallis-Wright of the Boston Symphony Orchestra.

Chris' gaze narrowed. "And you want to know about Strahan?"

"You were there at that meeting. You heard his name on the list. As I recall," she grinned in gentle accusation, "you were one of his most vocal supporters."

"And *you* were totally against the assignment. Changed your mind?"

She sighed, sliding into one of three chairs in the room, the only one free of debris. "What can I say? It's an assignment. Bill made that very clear—in front of all of you. I can't deny that the thought of this feature still goes against my grain, but I'm trying. Believe me, I am."

Chris had no way of knowing that those particular efforts were limited to the other four and excluded Strahan entirely.

"I believe you, Nia. OK," he rubbed his hands together, then perched before her on the corner of his desk. "Daniel Strahan. Everything I know about him?"

"Everything."

"What do you know already?"

She knew that he loved lobster and steak, medium-rare, that he was great for scrubbing broiler pans and dislodging jammed book cartons from behind the steering wheels of Volvos, that he drove a sporty maroon Datsun and liked to read—and that when he touched her she melted.

"I know that he coaches the New England Breakers, that he's six feet four and weighs somewhere around one hundred ninety." All bone and sinew, she elaborated from personal examination. But, of course, she couldn't tell Chris *that.*

"OK. We start from scratch." Folding his arms

across his chest, Chris frowned. "You know something? I'm not sure I know all that much."

"Give me what you've got." Anything would be better than nothing, she mused, particularly as she was beginning to feel incredibly guilty at the deception.

"I think he must be close to forty. No. Not quite. Thirty-eight or thirty-nine." He made the mental calculations, working forward from Daniel's playing years. "Bachelor, obviously."

"Obviously." She pinched in her lips with wry humor.

"He's coached the Breakers for four seasons now, the last two winning ones."

"What did he do before he coached? He didn't go right up from the bench, did he?"

Chris shook his head. "There were several years in between there when he scouted for the team." His brow furrowed as he dug into his memory. "I think I recall reading that he went back to school."

"Really?" Daniel had mentioned this. An occasional course—that was what he'd said. Was he possibly working toward a more formal postgraduate degree in psychology? "But you don't know any of the details."

Again, Chris defaulted. "Sorry, Nia. There must be some bio that appeared in the papers at the time he was named head coach. Have you checked?"

"The microfilm room is my next stop." She grinned. "I'm trying the shortcuts first. Do you think there would be anything in the Breakers' yearbook? Have you got the new one?"

"At home," he acknowledged apologetically. "I'll bring it in tomorrow. I've also got a copy of the team schedule and, hey, if you'd like, I'll go through my old sports magazines. They've *got* to have stuff on Strahan."

"Would you, Chris?" She brightened. "That would be great!"

"Sure thing, love." He paused to study her closely, then eyed her askance. "Say, this is strictly business, isn't it? You're not about to be turned on by six feet of well-toned muscle, are you?"

Her brittle laugh was a poor denial of his low-growled suggestion. "Don't be absurd, Chris! You know how I feel about anything to do with basketball."

"I know that your ex was involved with the Breakers, so it might be fair to say that you've got it in for the game. Still . . . there was a ring of excitement in your voice a minute ago. And, if it's not to do with the old hoop and ball, it must have to do with—"

"Wrong, friend," she laughed, gaining better control of herself. "Try again." Her grin was a challenge to occupy him while she engaged in a minute of self-reproach. She'd simply *have* to do something about her tone of voice, that tone of voice inspired solely by Daniel Strahan. Twice, now, it had nearly betrayed the emotion that nagged at her.

"I know!" Chris put on a scowl. "You're trying to make me jealous."

"You?" She stood, prepared to leave at the first appropriate moment. Chris had come far too close to the truth for comfort.

"Yeah," he drawled. "You know how I love basketball and you're just dying to dangle those free tickets he gives you right under my nose."

Nia drew alongside him and put her arm around his shoulder. "Now, would I do that to you?" she asked. "I'll make a deal with you. If you bring in that material you've promised tomorrow, I'll *give* you those free tickets . . . *if* he hands them out."

"Pretty lady," Chris lit up, "you're got yourself a deal!"

If only other things could be resolved as easily, she mused later. With Daniel Strahan monopolizing the back of her mind all day, nothing seemed to work out smoothly.

The microfilm room, with its single viewer, had been appropriated by a young staffer whose plea that she was already far behind schedule fell on Nia's sympathetic ear. After all, Nia reasoned, her own research wasn't exactly an emergency. In fact, she doubted she should even be doing it on company time . . . since she would not be using it for official purposes.

And therein lay a world of guilt. She had, despite any stretch of the imagination, led Chris on. When she should have been appealing to him for a suitable replacement for Daniel in the *Eastern Edge* feature, she had knowingly let Chris believe her inquiries to be on the up-and-up. Oh, they were on the up-and-up, all right, but it was a very personal high she courted.

She wanted to know Daniel, to understand *him* as he claimed to want to understand *her.* The difference was principally in his willingness to be known. While she had talked to him with a remarkable lack of inhibition, he had revealed very little of a truly personal nature to her. So, reporter-at-heart that she was, she would seek out the information on her own.

It was, unfortunately, hard to come by. After striking out at the microfilm department, she raced to a nearby bookstore, where she spent a full hour browsing through any and every publication, first downstairs in hardback, then up in paper, that dealt in any form or fashion with basketball. There was no shortage of life stories on some of the current big stars of the game. But on Daniel Strahan? Nothing.

She returned to her office after stopping to pick up a fast chicken salad sandwich to go, then munched on it at her desk and reviewed what she *had* learned. Daniel Strahan had originally come from Oregon, had made his mark at Stanford and been the Breakers' first-round draft pick in his senior year. He'd moved directly to Boston and had remained with the team until his retirement after ten years of frontline basketball. In his later playing years, he had been bothered by a troublesome knee, but, otherwise, he had been regarded as one of the Breakers' outstanding forwards. Period. Nothing more recent, save passing references to the success of the New England Breakers "under Head Coach Daniel Strahan." No details on Daniel.

No personal dirt. Nothing. Nia's violet gaze grew darker in frustration. For this she had wasted the better part of the morning?

With a low oath and a spate of noble resolutions, she set off to meet with Arthur Wallis-Wright. Things had to get better; Symphony Hall was a favorite spot of hers. Of course, she had been here primarily for special concerts: a notable flute soloist, a small Baroque ensemble—but how different could the atmosphere be under the auspices of the first violinist and concertmaster of the Boston Symphony Orchestra?

Very different, she discovered upon being ushered into a stark room where the maestro had been practicing. She was totally ignored until the double bars, at which point the musician lowered the instrument from its niche beneath his chin, tucked it as a security blanket under his arm, and proceeded to toy with his bow strings for the duration of the interview.

After ten minutes of the distracting fidgeting, Nia felt that *she* was stretched taut. Forcing herself to remain poised as she explained the feature and what she wanted to achieve with it, she then asked several basic questions, made another appointment, this time to meet the violinist at his Brookline home, and fled. It was an instant relief to emerge once more into the brisk air of Huntington Avenue.

Paul Kiley, the first man she'd interviewed for the eligible easterner feature, had cast aside his initial wariness during that spontaneously prolonged first interview, but Wallis-Wright had remained awkward throughout. Nia's attempts to relax him had been in vain; she had been unable to put him at ease. Perhaps she had caught him on a particularly tense day; she had gathered that he would be conducting the orchestra that night in place of the ailing regular. That kind of pressure would distract anyone, she decided in his favor, half wishing he had thought simply to call her and postpone their meeting. He had been very proper and cordial, though, in spite of his nervousness. Perhaps he was always this way. Perhaps she would be able to work through that outer shield of formality next time, to find the man whom Bill Austen and the wizards upstairs had thought fit to classify as an "eligible easterner." Perhaps the Wallis-Wright type appealed to some women. . . .

Needing to clear her head, Nia opted out of taking the streetcar directly back to the office. Buttoning her reefer to her neck and burying her hands deep in her pockets, she struck out toward the imposing granite gathering of the Christian Science Center. Its reflecting pool had always fascinated her, mirroring as it did not only the heavens above but their climatic moods as well.

Though bounded by buildings on nearly three sides, the spot was relatively exposed. Pulling up her collar, she huddled more deeply into her coat as she watched the wind's chill create a broad expanse of ripples on the pool's fluid surface. There was a serenity here, regardless of the weather, a sense almost of communion that affected her each time she came. It never failed to soothe her.

Perched on the stone rim of the pool, she

sighed. Whether in spite, or because, of the peacefulness of the setting, her mind turned to Dan. She had enjoyed herself last night far more than she had in months. There was an ease in talking with him, even in the challenge of getting him to talk about himself. He was intelligent; she sensed an untapped reserve of knowledge on topics far beyond basketball.

But basketball was his life just now; that alone put him beyond her reach. Nor did her mishandling of his role in the feature story please her, and she still had Bill to face on that score.

Should she have been more formal herself? Should she have rigidly clung to her role as writer and left the arena that day at Daniel's first refusal to cooperate? But then she would never have known the headiness of his kiss and the richness of his embrace. Dead-end street that he was, Daniel Strahan made her feel good. She liked that.

Before her eyes, the stucco surface of the pool grew glassily smooth for an instant. With a flash of clarity, Nia reached a tentative conclusion. What harm was there in enjoying Daniel Strahan? She knew there was nowhere to go. It would only take one road trip to remind her that this was a passing pleasure. If her expectations were low, there would be no hurt, no disappointment. So why not relax and take him in stride? After all, if by some remote possibility he did end up in the pages of *Eastern Edge* he would be no different from any other of the people she'd interviewed over the years. On the other hand, if she let instinct rule her desire to keep his privacy intact, there could surely be no problem with seeing him every so often. If *he* wanted that. A big "if." An "if" that only time would resolve.

As she stood and slowly walked along the open mall toward Copley Square, she recalled his final words of the night before. "I'll give you a call," he had said, but his meaning had been vague. Had it been a promise to reach a decision on the article—or had it been the anticipation of something far more personal? That he had been affected by her, drawn to her, was clear. However, there was nothing she could do but wait until he chose to make his move. In the meantime, she vowed, she would unbend and enjoy her life as she had before Daniel Strahan's appearance.

Pleased at having settled something in her mind, Nia walked more briskly, skirting the Boston Public Library, then ducking into the subway stop. When she emerged into daylight at Government Center, she felt pleasantly calm. It was in this refreshed frame of mind that she returned to the office and withstood several hectic hours of meetings and phone calls and desk work without a murmur. Things were flowing smoothly once more; her satisfied smile attested to it.

The sun had just begun to set beyond the Charles River when she finally took the elevator to the ground floor and crossed the plaza toward the subway. As she had intended—and as she very often did—she had missed the worst of the rush hour by staying the hour or so later at the office. The crowd was thinning now, and she easily found a seat for the ride to Harvard Square.

Once there, her luck held. Ironically, now that there were no raindrops to dodge, the bus was waiting at the curb for her, closing its door behind her as soon as she was safely aboard and speeding her home. A quick glance at her watch brought a sweet surge of pleasure; she would have time to change and make dinner before the start of the pregame show. What was *he* doing now? Had he eaten in that same little restaurant today—perhaps the special had been scampi? She could almost smell it!

Her broiled scrod was a far cry from scampi, and the silence that served as her dinner companion was a far cry from Daniel's lively presence. But nonchalance was the word. She relaxed, read the mail, even glanced at the article she'd brought home with her to edit. With an eye ever on the clock, however, she flipped on the small television set at precisely the moment that the station's commentator introduced Daniel.

What followed was an awakening! There was Daniel, looking very familiar and as handsome as ever, responding to questions in the deep flow of verbal velvet she had come to expect. But his manner was wholly different from anything *she* had ever seen in him. There was a professional polish to him, a practiced evenness, an ultimate preparedness for each and every question. It was almost as if he'd seen the script before, memorized it, and now spewed back pat answers without a flicker of concentration.

"The Breakers beat the Bullets for their tenth straight win the other night," the commentator began, stating the obvious for the benefit of the home audience. "How does the team react to the streak?"

"We take it one game at a time. The Bullets are a strong team, one of the strongest in the league. They may well make the playoffs this year. In that sense, the win pleased us." Not a blink or a smile broke his placid expression.

"You're still working without Walker and Barnes?"

"That's right."

"Can you continue to hold up without them?"

"Our backups are good and getting stronger with each game. They're more rested than some of the regulars. It's taken a rethinking of some of our usual plays, but we're adjusting to the loss pretty well. I'll be starting Harwood and Flagg at forward, Rockowski at center, Jones and Fitzgerald at guard. They're a tough five."

"Any special strategy for defense in tonight's game?"

"We're focusing on Montrose. When he gets the ball, we'll go to double-teaming."

"There's been talk that Jones' game is too personal."

"Gunner is a shooting guard. It's what he does best. I think he's aware of the rest of the team; he moves around."

"Will Watts see any playing time tonight? I understand he pulled a muscle in practice today."

"He's suited up. If we need him, he'll play."

"What about Houston? They've got their own streak of six going. Can you beat them?"

"I hope so."

"Is it too early to break out the bubbles for the Atlantic Division title?"

"Yes. Things could always turn around, but we'll be working tonight to make sure they don't."

"And that's all we can ask." The camera pulled back to encompass their handshake. "Thanks for talking with us, Dan, and good luck tonight."

A half-smile from Daniel. "My pleasure, Johnny."

That was it. All of three minutes of rapid-fire dialogue that said absolutely nothing! If Christopher Daly thought such interviews were "brilliant" or "concise," he was a starry-eyed idealist! Nia turned away from the set, only now aware that her heartbeat was faster than usual. That was the last kind of interview she'd expected Dan to give. But why? The more she considered it, the more sense it made. Daniel had revealed nothing—nothing to antagonize either fans, players or the opposition. As team spokesman, that was his job. His comments had been benign enough to preclude offense on any front.

Yet Nia had taken Daniel Strahan as a man of very distinct opinions. Was she disappointed in his mechanical performance here? On the contrary—to her astonishment, she was actually pleased! If this was the public Daniel Strahan, the one whose face the press saw, then she had, without realizing it at the time, seen something deeper. Dan had never given her stock answers like those she'd heard from him tonight. He had *reacted* to her! That thought was strangely flattering.

From a distant shore of consciousness came the

steady cheer of the crowd, its roar setting off the old, familiar anguish of memory within her. David. It was still his game. It was still a cruel game, making demands on its participants that normal relationships simply could not handle.

The crowd stilled for the deep baritone of a local entertainer. But Nia's mind was once more on the past, recalling the unhappiness that the sounds of the game represented. What did the players' wives feel when their husbands spent half of each season on the road? How did *they* survive?

On impulse she turned the set off. Well, she reasoned, she'd seen Daniel, and that had been her sole purpose in watching. Putting up with the clamor of the game was still something she resented.

She did, however, buy the newspaper on her dash through the Square unusually early the next morning. Her hands were full, juggling her pocketbook and the material she'd brought home the night before, as she struggled to read the sports page against the relentless interference of the wind. Her feet knew the way of the well-worn walk beneath the high archways into Harvard Yard. Her destination was the Widener Library; she had the *Eastern Edge* pass in her purse. Today she was taking no chance on microfilms at the office. Widener had several machines and opened early enough for her to do her work and still get into Boston before her absence created a stir.

The Breakers had won again! It had been a closer game this time, with only a two-point spread at the final bell, but it was nonetheless a win! Feeling a sudden surge of energy, Nia crushed the paper against her and took the tall flight of stone steps to the library's front door without a pause. Once inside, she read the article in its entirety, her eye sharpening each time it caught sight of his name.

All told, she spent two hours viewing microfilms before she was satisfied with their yield. When she left the library her arms were laden with photocopies of several of the more substantive articles she'd found, plus issues of magazines that had carried articles about the team during Daniel's playing years. She would carefully comb through these at the office. What with the newer magazines that Chris had promised, she might actually learn something.

Unfortunately, she had time only to pick up Chris' bounty on her spring by his office, then lay the entire collection in a random heap on her own desk before a call from Bill came through.

"On the double, Nia!" he summoned her over the intra-office line. "We've got a problem."

"A problem?" she echoed him, perplexed.

"Mahoney."

Just one word. But it had the power to send a twist of anxiety through her.

"Uh-oh. I'll be right there." Within minutes she was in Bill's office, leaning wide-eyed over his desk to study the document that had been delivered a short time earlier. "A *subpoena?*" she exclaimed in disbelief.

Bill let the folded blue paper fall flat on his desk.

"He's reopening the suit. This paper names you, me, Bruce and *Eastern Edge* as codefendants."

"I can't believe this." She shook her head, stunned. "I thought he dropped all thought of a suit after our apology appeared in print."

"Evidently he feels it wasn't enough."

"At this late date? My article appeared over two years ago. What's he been doing all this time that now he's suddenly so concerned about libel?" As astonishment turned to anger, Nia's temper sought an outlet.

"Sit down, Nia, and take it easy. It's not that much of a mystery."

"Then *you* explain it to me," she demanded, but she took a seat as he had suggested and braced her arms tensely.

"Jimmy Mahoney has been the mayor of Boston for three years now. He's up for reelection in November."

"What does *that* have to do with *this?*" She pointed an accusing finger at the subpoena. "The article is ancient history."

"Nothing is ancient history in an election year." Bill chided her short-sightedness. "Particularly in *this* city. If Mahoney can find a straw horse to divert attention from other issues—more shaky issues, such as the local tax rate or compulsory auto insurance premiums or the disabilities commission—he'll ride it for all it's worth."

"At our expense?" she asked, finally beginning to understand.

"Yes."

With a deep breath of resignation, Nia folded her hands in her lap. "So . . . what happens now?"

"Now we honor this subpoena and freely give the depositions that Mahoney's counsel is demanding."

"When?"

"A week from next Monday. That gives you ten days to gather together any information—records, files, documents—that you used at the time. You had it put together once before, didn't you?"

"Yeah," she snorted. "I didn't have to use it . . . then."

"Well, you may not have to use it now. He could still change his mind again. Just . . . be prepared. Have everything fresh in your mind. OK?"

"OK."

She stood up to leave with the distinct feeling that the bubble she'd floated on this morning had suddenly burst. Sensing her distress, Bill walked her to the door.

"Are you all set to go to Pennsylvania next week?"

"Uh-huh." Her voice held only forced interest. "I'll be leaving either Tuesday or Wednesday. Back on Friday."

He nodded. "Everything else going all right?"

"Strahan won't work with us. Can you find a replacement?"

Though it was a totally spontaneous outburst, Nia couldn't have chosen a better time for her announcement had she planned the entire thing. At this moment she had Bill's sympathy. Aware of her distress on the other matter, he wasn't about to press her.

"You're sure?"

"Pretty sure."

"OK. I'll discuss it up above and try to come up with someone. If he changes his mind in the meantime, you let me know."

"I will." She smiled for the first time since entering his office those few short but disturbing minutes ago. "And . . . thanks, Bill." The thanks was for his understanding. Sensing that, he sent her on her way with a modest nod.

With Priscilla out of the office on an assignment for the morning, Nia was left alone with dreary thoughts of the subpoena in Bill's possession. She recalled the original mention of a libel suit two years ago. At that time, both Bill and Bruce McHale had assured her that nothing would come of the suit. Somehow she felt shakier now. Was it that, having built her career so much higher, she had that much more to lose? After all, hers *had* been the by-line on the exposé. . . .

Brooding seemed useless. There was nothing she could do yet. Without searching the file cabinet, she knew her records to be intact. It would simply be a matter of bringing the file home and reviewing it at some point before a week from Monday. She had time; the weekend before would suffice. That way, everything would be fresh in her mind.

It was with the best of intentions that Nia

turned to the messages on her desk. She answered each with determined interest, making side trips to both the art and copy departments on demand. Indeed, she managed to divert her thoughts from the pending lawsuit to the May issue of *Eastern Edge* for a time. But that more ugly issue hung there quietly, a threatening cloud in an otherwise optimistic sky.

Word spread quickly among the magazine's staff. At noon, two friends from the accounts department stopped by to wisk her off for a morale-boosting lunch. Food, however, was the last thing on Nia's mind. She graciously declined their invitation, returning to her work only after she had extracted the promise of a rain check.

Chris met the same fate shortly after when he stopped by on a similar mission. "Come on, Nia. It would do you good. We'll show the world and Jimmy Mahoney that we're not easily scared."

Her smile was one of gratitude for his support. "Thanks, Chris, but I think I'll work a while longer. I haven't even touched the things you brought in for me." Indeed, she hadn't. She felt a strange reluctance to dirty any of the Strahan information with wayward thoughts of libel.

Chris nodded his understanding. "We'll make it another day, how's that? Oh, and you won't forget your part of the bargain, will you?"

"No, Chris," she replied in a sweetly docile tone. "I won't."

It was closer to one-thirty when the antidote to her mood finally arrived. Hand cramped from the repeated rewriting of a particularly troublesome piece, she wearily raised her eyes from the paper to feast on the unexpected sight of Daniel, standing straight and tall at her office door.

six

DANIEL!" SHE EXCLAIMED, A RESPONSE which was becoming a habit whenever he appeared where she didn't quite expect him. "What are *you* doing here?" Instantly, she felt better.

He smiled devilishly. "Oh, practice was over and I had nothing to do. Thought I'd take a ride into Boston to see what was cookin'."

"Don't ask." She grimaced before she could quite help herself.

All traces of humor left Daniel's face as he sensed something wrong. "Trouble?"

"Oh . . . nothing." But she hesitated too long.

"Listen." Looking around, he saw signs of her co-workers returning from lunch. "I was hoping to get here earlier and take you to lunch, but you've probably already eaten. Is there somewhere you could get coffee while *I* eat?"

Nia scowled in a playful attempt to put aside her worry. "You seem obsessed with hunger. If I'd imagined you thought of nothing but basketball, I stand corrected." Reaching for her purse, she had made her decision. *This* was someone with whom she wanted to have lunch! "I know just the restaurant. It's in the Marketplace. I've got to visit it anyway to review it for the June issue."

"My issue?" He cast her a sidelong glance which she returned in kind. No further word was said on that score. Rather, Daniel put his hand lightly at her back as they walked toward the elevator. "Why do I have the sudden feeling I'm being used?" he asked, but his voice was filled with fun.

"You are!" she returned his gentle teasing. "It's either *that* or nothing, right now!"

"I'll take it!" he quipped instantly, capturing her hand in his larger one and swinging her before him into the elevator.

They said little to one another during the descent, even less as they walked through the City Hall plaza toward the Faneuil Hall Market. Nia derived quiet comfort from his presence, untold strength from the protective grip of his fingers. He had come at just the right time—how could he have known?

At the entrance to the Marketplace, he came to a halt, oblivious to the few heads that turned their way in recognition. "OK, babe," he surveyed the long brick-paved mall with its double cordon of shops and eateries. "Which one will it be?"

Nia pointed to a second level of windows overlooking the mall. "Rosemary's Thyme. We go in over here." Leading the way, she entered an open foyer off which several shops branched, then tackled the very clearly marked flight of open-planked stairs. At the top of its gentle spiral, Daniel stepped forward to secure a table, speaking softly to the hostess and gesturing toward the far end of the restaurant.

"I have just the table, Mr. Strahan." The hostess beamed with admiration. "It's being cleared right now. Would you care to wait in the bar?"

"Thank you, but we'll wait here." He smiled cordially, bringing Nia beside him to the shaded alcove just beyond the hostess' station. Belatedly, he thought of her thirst. "I'm sorry, Nia. Would *you* like something to drink?"

"No, no. This is fine. I'll have something when we sit down." She narrowed her gaze in the direction of the hostess. "I'm curious to see how long they keep us waiting. Speed of service is a definite consideration in any rating."

"Wait a minute," he growled. "You're not going to take out your little black notebook and start making notes with the air of a super-sleuth, are you?"

Nia's laughter was light and she was far more relaxed than she'd felt all morning. The image he'd created was too much! Daniel, in turn, clearly enjoyed her laugh. "Do you do this often?"

"I usually wear my Sherlock Holmes hat."

"I'm serious. Do you rate restaurants on a regular basis?"

"Not really. It's kind of a rotating thing that we each do once in a while. With everyone on the staff taking his turn, no one stands that great a risk of recognition."

"I was wondering about that. Isn't there a danger you *will* be recognized and given preferential treatment?"

She crinkled her nose. "I have a nondescript face . . . and I keep a pretty low profile. They don't seem to recognize me." Pausing to grin, she turned the tables on him. "Actually, *you're* the one in danger of being recognized. Weren't you worried when you gave your name to the hostess?"

"I didn't *have* to give her my name," he whispered in a half-groan.

"Uh-oh. No wonder we're in hiding back here."

"It has its advantages."

"Oh?" She didn't resist the arm that snaked about her waist and pressed her close. Nor did she balk when he kissed her lightly. The feel of him was divine. "And what was that for?"

"For coming to lunch with me."

"I was hungry."

"You?"

Interference came in the form of a faintly awe-filled "Excuse me? Mr. Strahan? Your table is ready."

Daniel gave Nia a final squeeze as she stepped in front of him to follow the hostess. Walking before him, she was unaware that Daniel had fallen behind, far behind, until she reached their corner table and looked around. Her escort was across the room and shaking hands with a rotund gentleman who had risen from his seat to pat Daniel on the back. More than one curious gaze followed the showy gesture.

"I'm sorry," the hostess apologized to Nia on behalf of her overeager patron. "That must be very annoying to you."

"It's all right." Nia smiled with a touch of sadness at the realization that this was all part of Daniel's life. She took the seat that faced the body of the restaurant, which would leave Daniel's back as a shield against further interruption.

The table stood beside a full-length window, affording them a bird's-eye view of the Marketplace. It was here that Nia's eye held, absently following the passage of browsing visitors to the mall until, after being stopped a second time en route, Daniel finally joined her.

His own apology was firmly etched upon his face. He seemed truly disturbed and just a bit angry, if the working muscle of his jaw was any indication.

"You can pan the clientele here for lack of personal consideration." His eyes were hard in censure. "They see that I'm with a woman, they know that I must be here to eat my own lunch, yet they feel totally justified in stopping me."

"Do you know either of them?"

"Hell, no!" He kept his voice low in caution.

"You were gracious."

"I have to be. That's what's sometimes so frustrating. They're obviously Breakers fans. I can be diplomatic about excusing myself as quickly as possible, but I can't ignore them completely. It's all part of the game."

The sudden appearance at their table of a young boy brought both heads quickly his way.

He looked to be ten or eleven, wore a tie and jacket, was dark-haired and pale, and seemed to be utterly uncomfortable. "Dan . . ." he began hesitantly, ". . . could I please have your autograph?" Like a child first learning to walk and barreling on until the nearest wall stopped him, this boy talked slowly at first but with gaining momentum until one word raced after the other. "My Mom and Dad and me are here from Bangor for the weekend. I've got to go to the doctor this afternoon, but we've got tickets for tonight's game. Will you sign this?" Running out of breath, he stopped. In his hand was a cocktail napkin.

Something about the child struck Nia as heartrending. Was it his pallor? His timidity? The fact that he had come down from Maine in search of medical care? Alarmed, her eyes flew to Daniel's.

He must have seen it too, for he smiled his warmest, most genuine smile for the child. "Sure, son. I tell you what." He put an arm around the boy's shoulder to turn him back toward the hostess. "You go and ask that woman for a postcard of the restaurant. Then bring it back to me and I'll sign it for you." The boy left instantly.

"What if they don't *have* a postcard?" Nia asked, suddenly terrified that the child might be disappointed.

"They will. They always do. They may not put them on open display for everyone to pick up, but she'll find one somewhere."

Sure enough, the boy returned to proudly present precisely what Daniel had sent him for. Daniel took a pen from the inner pocket of his blazer, asked the boy his name, and proceeded to write a personal message on the back of the card.

The child's eyes were rewardingly bright when Daniel handed it back to him. "Thanks, Dan. Boy, wait 'til my friends see this!" he whispered hoarsely, then turned and retreated to where his parents sat anxiously. His mother mouthed a very grateful "thank you" to Dan, reinforcing Nia's fear.

"Do you think he's ill?" she asked softly.

Daniel shrugged. "Could be. Could be something minor. I'm always affected more by kids, anyway." He spoke as though to himself. "They're so innocent in their requests. And you know that, whether it's me or John Doe from the local 'Y' team, the boy will treasure that card."

"You like children?"

"They're often more sincere *and* more loyal."

"What about that twelve-year-old who swears down at you from just above the tunnel . . . ?" Teasingly, she reminded him of his past complaint.

Dan's lips quirked in renewing good-humor. "That's no kid. That's a twelve-year-old monster." Taking a pause, he looked across the table, deeply into her eyes. "What about you, Nia?"

"What *about* me? I'm no monster—"

"Something's bothering you. It was there in your eyes when I showed up at your office. I can still see it hiding behind a host of distractions."

"You're too perceptive, do you know that?" she asked, disconcerted.

"So I've been told. It's part of my personality. I'm afraid I can't do anything to change it."

"Is that why you're studying psychology?"

"You're skirting the issue again, Nia," he chided, having just done as much himself. *"Have* you got a problem?"

"Oh, it's really nothing." Frowning, she looked down at the crisp white linen and the sparkling bone china atop it. "One of my articles has caused a stir. That's all."

"Isn't that good? A stir is better than . . . nothing. . . ."

She chuckled. "Well put. And usually correct. But not in this case."

"And what makes this case so special?"

She eyed him levelly: "Two things. Jimmy Mahoney. And libel."

"Jimmy Mahoney . . . as in *mayor* . . . and libel . . . as in *suit?"*

"Correct on both counts."

"That bad?"

Sending him a sharp glance that confirmed the worst, Nia turned to examine the menu. "We've got to order different things," she softly instructed him in the fine art of the restaurant critic. "You choose what *you* want, then I'll pick something from another column."

"Can we share the end results?" he asked, finally ordering chilled sweet-and-sour salmon to Nia's crabmeat quiche.

Smiling at the intimacy, she recalled the solid feel of him in the alcove earlier; now she had the comforting knowledge of his emotional support. "As long as we don't drop it all on the table in the process. Some foods are pretty tricky that way—you know, spaghetti, peas . . ."

"I get the picture," he drawled. "We haven't ordered any of those. Beside that, I'm very neat. I even waited table at college."

"And *I've* seen those lovely dining hall presentations. The kitchen makes plenty of extra to compensate for what falls on the floor."

Daniel's laugh warmed her, as had the unexpected glimpse at his past. "It wasn't *that* bad. I was better than most—I toss things pretty well."

"Like lettuce?" She recalled the green head that had come to within inches of her kitchen ceiling one night.

He smiled. "That, too."

"Now tell me you cut your teeth backhanding oranges into the fruit bowl. . . ."

"It was more like eggs into the frying pan. My mother wasn't terribly thrilled. Backhanding—" He redirected the talk with a straightforward grin. "Where did you pick up that phrase? Is it a hold-over . . . or did you actually watch the game last night?"

She felt a fleeting pain at the reference to David. But she was grateful for it. In Daniel's presence she needed firm reminders of what he was, and David was as good a one as any. "I read the paper this morning," she confessed evenly. "And I did catch your pregame interview."

"What did you think?"

As she struggled to find an appropriately innocuous word, she thought she recognized the dance of amusement in Daniel's deep brown gaze. "It was . . . well handled."

His humor was more blatant now and held a challenge. "Anything else?"

"Why do I sense that you're laughing at me?"

He did laugh, aloud. "You're adorable—trying so hard to find the right word to describe something that was, to be blunt, insipid."

"Did *I* call it that?" she chided lightly.

"You're too polite. *I* supplied the word. Is it a poor choice?"

She hesitated. "Well, you didn't say very much, did you?"

"Nope."

"Which was exactly what you had intended to do."

"Right."

"So I repeat—it was well handled."

Daniel dipped his head. "Thank you."

Even before the entrées arrived, Nia felt revived. On this day, at least, Daniel Strahan was the best thing that had come along. It was almost worth talking basketball . . . to avoid that other, more disturbing issue.

"I think I can understand how you'd get into trouble doing anything but what you did," she reasoned. "How is the salmon?"

"Not bad." He concentrated on his mouthful, moving it across his taste buds in careful analysis before swallowing. "Just firm enough. Very good. Not too sweet. Well balanced. Could be just a little warmer." He frowned. "Take that question on

Jones." Nia followed the conversational flip-flop easily. "I couldn't very well tell the television audience that Gunner has been fined more than once for monopolizing the ball. That's between him and me. Certain things have to be kept private . . . for the overall morale of the team, if nothing else. It's almost like a family." His gaze grew more ardent. "You don't bad-mouth your own kin."

"Tell me about yours," she asked more gently. She felt so close to him. It mattered very much to her to learn about his past.

"My family?" His voice was quiet, his ardor controlled. "There's not much to tell."

"Anything's better than nothing."

"You're sure you're not taking notes?" he shot grimly, suddenly untrusting, as though he too remembered their inherent conflicts.

"Only on the salad. My dressing is a little heavy. What do you think?"

Willing to accept her lightness as innocence, he paused to sample his tomato and endive. "Mmmm. A little."

As he fell silent, Nia wondered whether something about his past made him uncomfortable. She really knew nothing but the bare sketch she'd pieced together. Was there some skeleton in his closet? Was there a reason for his fierce instinct for privacy? Or was he simply wary of her still?

"You grew up in Oregon?" she ventured cautiously.

His gaze shot up. "So you *have* been at work."

"Well, *you* won't tell me anything. I guess I'm just a natural snoop."

"What are you looking for?"

"I want to know about *you.*"

When he asked "Why?" there was a distant chill in his voice.

Time seemed to circle back on itself. It was almost as if she had been returned to his office, to that very first day they'd met. Had they come no further?

She answered his question with one of her own, one much softer and brimming with a sadness she could never have expressed had it not come from her heart.

"You don't trust me, do you?"

His eyes held hers in a smoothly glittering challenge. "Should I?"

"Yes."

"Why?"

"That's a foolish question. . . ." In the back of her mind was the memory of a similar exchange. Then he had said he trusted her, yet he questioned her now. Why? The extent of her hurt startled her.

"I'm asking it anyway." He held firm.

Nia let her fork fall to the plate, a victim of disinterest. Without Daniel's warmth and approval she felt infinitely lonely. "You should trust me . . . because . . . I care. And besides," she couldn't resist a tentative grin on the outside chance that it might cajole him into better humor, "you have to understand that my motives are pure. It's the force of sheer feminine curiosity that drives me. By keeping everything about you in such deep, dark secrecy, you've made me all the more intrigued.

Or," she felt a sudden suspicion, "was that the point all along?"

"It wasn't," he had thawed suddenly, "but now that I think of it, it's a pretty good tactic for holding a woman's interest. Here I thought I was such a superior strategist . . ."

"Daniel . . ." she hummed a playful warning as her own tactic worked, to her delight, in the form of a devastatingly masculine smile.

"Yes, Nia," he growled, "what is it you'd like to know?"

"You're serious?" Excitement did strange things to the corners of her lips.

"Sure. Why not? If I see my life story smeared all over *Eastern Edge* I can always—" He caught himself before he said the word, but she heard it nonetheless.

"Sue." She filled in the blank with a shudder. "Go ahead. Say it. It certainly won't be the first time it's happened."

"Tell me about it, Nia—the thing with Mahoney. You *are* allowed to talk, aren't you? I mean, I wouldn't want you divulging any confidential information."

"I can talk." She *needed* to talk, to somehow express her frustration. "It's all a matter of public record, anyway."

"Already? I don't recall seeing anything in the papers."

"It was a long time ago. If you saw something then, you would probably have forgotten it by now. Nothing came of it . . . then."

"When was that?"

"Two years ago."

"Go on."

From the corner of her eye Nia saw the waitress approach. "Do you want dessert?" she asked in anticipation.

"I want you to talk to me."

"But I need your help on this, Dan. For the sake of my review . . ."

What had been a stage whisper rose to a normal speaking tone with the arrival of the waitress. Nia turned to the woman in utter innocence. "Are there any house specialties you can recommend for dessert?"

Daniel coaxed Nia into discussion over a fresh strawberry tart and mint chocolate mousse, respectively. "What happened two years ago to get Mahoney's dander up?"

"I wrote an article in honor of the first anniversary of his swearing-in as mayor."

"Sounds nice enough. . . . Here," he held a forkful of tart her way and watched as she pressed her lips around the offering; only then did he slowly withdraw the fork.

"Mmmmm." But was it the freshness of the tart that was so satisfying . . . or the innate richness of its donor?

"You were saying . . . ?" he prodded.

"Unfortunately, there was nothing terribly nice about my article. I mean, it was well written and carefully researched. But it claimed a gross conflict of interest on the part of Jimmy Mahoney."

All playfulness forgotten, Dan frowned. "Wait a minute. I do remember something. Wasn't it about some piece of waterfront property?"

"Good memory, Professor," she quipped, impressed anew by his intellect. "As a lawyer in private practice before his election, Jimmy Mahoney was part-owner of a very large piece of prime development property. Within three months of his inauguration a huge complex was proposed for the site—a hotel, entertainment and shopping setup. The city granted the developers a significant tax break. Theoretically, it was a serious conflict of interest for the mayor."

"Theoretically," he agreed. "And that's what you reported?"

"Very vividly. . . . Here, you finish this." She thrust her mousse across the table, barely missing the rose-filled bud vase. "I'm not as hungry as I thought."

"Just relax, Nia. It can't be all that bad." He sampled the mousse as he continued. "Wasn't there a press conference at the time, a retraction based on some misunderstanding?"

"The misunderstanding occurred because Mahoney had failed to officially register the fact that he had divested himself of the property before taking office. The fact that he still knew the owners and the developer was a secondary issue, perhaps more a matter of poor judgment than a legal conflict of interest."

"You did publish a retraction."

"We certainly did! It satisfied him. Up until

now." As succinctly as possible, she related Bill Austen's theory on the force behind the revival.

A dark anger simmered in Dan's eyes. "Isn't that unethical—the arbitrary use of a suit like that?"

"It's a political strategy—and *you* know about strategies. He has every right in the world to do what he's doing. It may be unfair . . ." As the gist of the situation hit her anew, she shook her head in dismay. "I can't believe I've got to go through this again."

Daniel regarded her closely, his expression holding an understanding that more than justified her having discussed the lawsuit with him. Almost absently, he reached for the sterling silver pitcher left by the waitress and topped off their coffee cups. "Isn't this kind of thing unusual for a magazine like *Eastern Edge?* I somehow envision it as being unabrasive."

"Unabrasive is often dull, and dull doesn't sell. No, we purposely set aside one article in each issue that *is* an exposé, that deals with an issue that's potentially fiery. We try to present the facts without petty name-calling; a lawsuit is the last thing we want. In the case of my article, not only were the facts erroneous—through no fault of mine—but they were far from complimentary to one Jimmy Mahoney, and he has a lot of power in this city."

Both brows arched, Daniel rubbed the side of his nose. "On the one hand, I can understand his being upset. On the other hand, as a public figure, he might not want to continue with a weak libel suit."

"I certainly hope not. If Bill's theory is correct, Mahoney may not care about the outcome as long as the pretrial process evokes sympathy among the voters."

"And what's the worst that could happen to you, Nia?" he asked more softly, coaxing out her greatest fears.

"I don't even want to think about it." She rolled her eyes.

"Tell me—what's the worst?"

With a deep breath, she met his gaze. "The worst would be a libel suit in which *Eastern Edge* was forced to pay substantial damages to Jimmy Mahoney on the grounds that his character and career have been irreparably damaged. I assume that, though the publication does carry insurance against such an eventuality, should that happen Antonia Phillips will be looking for a new job."

"Which wouldn't be *so* terribly awful, would it?" His tone was gentle, protective in its way. Nia saw what he was trying to prove to her.

"No, Daniel, it wouldn't be the end of the world." She put the possibility in its proper perspective. "But it would set my career back some."

"You'd rebound," he declared with such conviction that she did feel better. "And *that* is the *worst.* Chances are it will never get to court. If Mahoney is using it for political purposes, he may not want to have it go to trial. What if he loses?" The point well taken, Nia smiled. "He may simply make a whole lot of noise about it—partly in the hope of frightening any other publication away from printing anything derogatory."

With a sigh, she nodded. "You're right, Dan. Everything you say makes sense. When you say it, I do believe that it will all work out. But . . . there's still going to be a mess in the process. How do I handle that?"

Reaching across the table, Daniel covered her tensed hand with his. "You'll keep cool and continue with your work. You'll do whatever preparation you have to do to present your case. You'll simply continue to do your best. Is there any alternative?"

Nia was suddenly conscious of how much better she felt about the libel suit than when Bill had popped it on her this morning. Perhaps the shock had simply worn off. More probably, talking it out with Dan had worked off the edge. How good it was to discuss things with him—he was so reasonable, so compassionate. It had been a long, long time since she had had a man's strength to fall back on in her own moments of weakness. Perhaps that was why she savored him all the more.

Under cover of his palm, she turned her own hand until her more slender fingers curled decisively around his. "Thanks, Dan," she drawled. "I needed that!" Her smile held humor . . . and something more. It was that same feminine aura emerging, and though the voice of experience cried out in warning, she selfishly ignored it.

Daniel's hand tightened almost imperceptibly. "Come on, Nia. Let me walk you back to the office."

They went back the way they'd come, this time more slowly, prolonging the pleasantness of being together. Daniel took her arm and drew it through his, holding her close to his side as they walked.

"You know that you've done it again, Daniel, don't you?" Nia teased him grudgingly. If only his shoulder weren't so inviting . . .

"Done what, babe?"

"Gotten me to talk about myself. You do it every time. I think you'll be a counselor one day."

"Perhaps." He smiled.

"You're very good at it. You make me feel so comfortable that I can't seem to stop the flow once it begins."

"I'm glad." He cast her a sidelong glance that held a tenderness far beyond "glad." If Nia was entralled with the day, Daniel was no less so.

"I wish you would feel free to talk with me," she began. "I really would like to learn what makes you tick. Did you always want to be a basketball player?"

Without further ado, he talked. "I always loved the game—from the day my dad put a net up on a tree at the edge of the driveway. It wasn't until later that I realized basketball could take me places."

"Such as . . . ?"

"Such as college, for starters. I went to Indiana on a full scholarship. Had I not gotten it, I doubt I would have been able to go on in school."

"Your parents must have been proud."

"They were. They are. Proud but stubborn."

They had reached the edge of the Government Center plaza and slowly headed down Tremont

Street. "What do you mean?" she asked, recalling something that had puzzled her once before.

"My father worked for the Postal Service for years; my mother taught piano. They scrimped and saved to give me everything they possibly could."

"You had no siblings?" She tipped her head up to his face.

"My mother gave birth to another child—a girl—three years after my birth. The baby died after eight months. At the time it was a mystery. Now they call it Sudden Infant Death Syndrome—SIDS. Anyway," he sighed, tucking her arm more tightly around his as though he needed the comfort of her presence, "they couldn't quite get themselves to go through it again. So they put all their energies into me."

"You must have been well loved."

"And spoiled." He smiled crookedly, barely disguising a certain sadness that wrenched Nia's heart. "They doted on me . . . until my mother got sick. Then it was up to my father and me to dote on her."

"What was wrong?"

"Nothing fatal. Simply a life's sentence of pain. She developed crippling arthritis. My father took her to doctor after doctor, but there's simply no cure." Frustration gripped his features, giving them a leaner slant as she looked up at him. "She had operation after operation, this joint replaced, then that. Although she's reached a plateau now, she's hopelessly confined to a wheelchair."

"How old were you when this all began?"

"I was a sophomore in high school. You can understand why I worked so hard to get good grades and win that scholarship. Even though it meant leaving Salem, the pride they felt made it worth it."

They were already a block up Beacon Street. "Where does the stubbornness fit in?" she asked, reminding him of his earlier claim.

Daniel looked fondly at her. "You are a pusher, aren't you?"

"Come on, Dan. We're almost at the office." Of necessity, their conversation would shortly have to end.

"OK. The stubbornness? *That* came when I signed my first contract and began to send money home. I quickly discovered that rather than using it on themselves, as I had hoped, they were banking every cent—to be left to their grandchildren one day." But there were no grandchildren. Would there ever be?

"That's a beautiful thought, Dan, but I can understand your frustration. Were you ever able to get around them?"

She'd never seen so cocky a grin. "Now . . . what do *you* think?"

"OK," she smiled, "what did you do?"

"I went back to Salem myself and *bought* them a little ranch-style house in the suburbs. I stood over the workers as they installed ramps. I threw out the old wheelchair and replaced it with a motorized one. And I bought them a van, fully equipped so that they could go wherever they wanted in comfort."

"That's great!"

"Yeah," he drawled grudgingly. "They still bank every blessed cent I send. But at least, when I see something they need, I know how to provide it."

"You must feel good about that." She beamed with pride in him.

"I do." He smiled more gently as he met her gaze. "Now if I could only do something about those grandchildren . . ."

They had reached her building, taken the elevator to her floor, and now ambled toward her office with shared reluctance. Nia felt that beyond even his patience and sympathy, Daniel had given her a greater gift today. It was a little slice of himself, a slice made all the more precious by the knowledge that very few people had ever received it. She had a friend—a very bright, handsome and sexy one.

With a deep sigh and a thud of resignation she dropped her purse on her chair. At that moment the phone rang, but their good-byes had not yet been said. After that last statement of Daniel's, a pregnant silence had settled over them. Though not awkward, it spoke of questions unasked, and so unanswered. Now Nia held up her finger to have Daniel wait while she quickly dispensed with the telephone call.

It was, ironically, a call from Thomas Reiss, a Vermont author, an "eligible easterner," with whom she had had an appointment scheduled for the following week. A conflict had arisen. Could the meeting possibly be rescheduled?

Nia swiveled in her chair to more fully face the wall calendar. A week from the following Tuesday—one day after the Mahoney hearing. Fine.

With the proper arrows from the old date to the new, she scrawled the name of Thomas Reiss in the allotted square. With a gracious "Thank you for calling, Mr. Reiss," she replaced the receiver and turned back to Daniel.

His eyes, however, did not budge from the array of papers and magazines spread randomly over her desktop. Following his gaze, she recalled too late the photocopies of newspaper articles, the books on sports, the self-explanatory magazine issues that, between her early morning jaunt to the library and the good graces of Christopher Daly, she had amassed.

Feeling strangely sheepish, as though she had been caught with her hand in the cookie jar, she began to explain. "Oh, don't mind these—" But the words stuck in her throat as Daniel's gaze met hers. The thunder of the blood suddenly pounding through her veins was nothing compared to the seething fury of his expression.

His jaw was clenched, his entire body rigid. Nia instantly realized his misinterpretation. She knew what was coming. Yet she was frozen by the force of his wrath. Her friend—she was on the verge of losing him!

He spoke with grating slowness, enunciating each word as he coated it with rage. "You're really going to do it, aren't you?"

In her fear, Nia hesitated a fraction of a second too long. For, having ground out his bitter message, he turned and was gone from the doorway. Stunned, she couldn't move. The brightness of her day had fled.

"Go after him, you dope!" Priscilla's whisper tore Nia from her trance. Their eyes met through the fern as Priscilla repeated her message. "Go on!"

Nia went. Dashing from the office, she was in time to see Daniel rounding the corner at the end of the corridor. "Dan!" she cried, then ran after him as quickly as her high-heeled pumps would allow. She caught up with him near the elevator. "Dan! Don't go! You're wrong!"

His gaze clung to the horizontal panel above the elevator doors. "Oh, yes," he sneered deeply, "I certainly was wrong!"

"It's not that way, Dan! Let me explain!"

"Oh, you can explain all right. The question is whether I can believe you."

"You've got to! I'm *not* doing the feature on you. Please believe that!"

He stared down at her with the indignance of a man who felt his intelligence had been insulted. "After what I just saw?"

"Yes!" The elevator arrived. Instinctively, she grabbed his arm to stop him from entering it. "Don't leave yet. . . ."

Her voice was a whisper; her eyes held gentle pleading. Daniel's gaze shifted from the taut fingers on his arm to the expectant faces in the elevator. He stood immobile for what seemed an eternity of inner agony. Slowly the elevator door slid shut.

"Find a private room," he growled, taking her arm into his grasp and ushering her back down the corridor, pausing only for her to check several offices that were already occupied.

"There's a supply room," she offered in a frantic whisper, fearful that he would change his mind and storm away. "It's the only thing!"

"Is this it?" he asked, thrusting open one of the few doors Nia hadn't already tried. It obviously was. Switching on the light, he let her precede him into a small room filled with reams of paper, folders, writing goods, mailing material, and a bevy of other decidedly inanimate objects. That was all he wanted. Privacy.

Turning his back on the door and leaning against it until it shut, he released her arm and crossed his own. "All right, Antonia. Talk."

Driven by voices of desperation within her, she faced him urgently. "I'm not using you for the feature, Daniel. I've already told Bill that!"

"Then why the material on your desk?" he seethed. "It sure as hell looked like you were researching someone to do with basketball. With your supposed aversion to the game—"

"Those *were* about you. I stopped at the library this morning. Chris brought in the magazines. But I wasn't researching you for my feature."

"Then why, Nia? Do you take me for an utter fool? I've been used by the media before. I thought I'd learned to recognize a con job when I saw it. This one stinks!"

"Bill is already finding a replacement," she went on, fighting the hurt that burgeoned inside. "I told him I couldn't use you. I've already told you that I didn't want to do the feature. Why won't you believe me?"

He stood like a clay giant, rigid and cynical. "You haven't yet given me any credible explanation for that stuff on your desk. If you're not doing the article on me, why the research?"

Nia wanted him to know the truth, but she didn't quite understand it herself. "I wanted to learn about you, Daniel. What more can I say?"

Pushing himself away from the door, he stalked her. She half-leaned, half-sat against a typing table, her hands white-knuckled around its edge. "You can tell me *why*, Nia!" he growled. "And don't give me that nonsense about innate curiosity and my refusing to tell you anything. You were certainly very successful today. You got what you wanted, didn't you?"

Pride kept her afloat before him. "Yes, damn it! You finally talked. You finally gave me a glimpse of the man behind the mask. I'm not sorry, Daniel!"

His initial anger had been gradually replaced with a fierceness that hinted at a far deeper emotion than fear of betrayal. Taking her shoulders in his hands, he brought her closer to him. "Now . . . what are you going to do with that information? That's what I'd like to know."

To her chagrin, her eyes filled with tears. "I'm going to use it to understand you, to appreciate you, to try to get to know you better."

"But why, damn it? *Why?*"

"I don't know!" she cried back, exasperated with her own inability to understand. "I just don't know!

You keep asking questions I can't answer! Maybe that's what I like about you, masochist that I am. You make me face things that I've refused to face. Through your eyes, I see things differently. As I talk with you, things become clearer." A solitary tear escaped to roll slowly over her cheekbone and her body trembled with emotion. His face had long since blurred in her fluid violet gaze, and she continued to lash out, ignorant of his softening. She had become a victim of emotion—an emotion she refused to face. "I didn't ask for you, damn it! And I don't know why I let you get to me this way! I sometimes wish I could scratch you out of my life the way I scratched you out of that feature story. *That* was the easy part!"

Breathless, she paused and slowly bowed her head. When she spoke again her own anger had been spent. Her voice was no more than a poignant whisper. "Go now, Dan. I just wanted you to know that I hadn't betrayed you. I . . . like you. Having met you and spent time with you has meant a lot to me. I'm sorry if I've caused your anger. . . ." Her words trailed off seconds before Daniel gently drew her against him. The hands that had so fiercely gripped her shoulders now crept around her back and pressed her into his warmth.

A low groan was the only sound that escaped his lips during those first few seconds. "Oh, Nia," he caressed her softly, "the anger you cause me has to do only with that hard head of yours. If only you had told me all of this sooner."

"Sooner?" she cried, pulling abruptly away from him. "Sooner? My God, I met you three days ago.

Three days ago! And I don't understand any of it! I don't know why I rush home to see you give an inane interview. I don't know why I spend my time wondering whether you're going to call. And I don't know why the devil I'm standing here telling you all this!"

She would have turned and fled had Daniel's full smile not stopped her. As it always did, it reached into her, drawing her nearer. "Confession is good for the soul," he growled, but in pleasure this time, as he enveloped her once more in the circle of his arms.

Unable to help herself, Nia buried her face deeper against him. "Oh, Daniel, why do you have this power over me?"

He forced a finger beneath her chin to tip her face back. "The power isn't one-sided, babe. I'm not exactly immune to you, either."

With that he kissed her. His lips offered the apology he felt, as hers returned the words in silence. Though Nia wasn't quite sure of the limits of her feelings, she knew that Daniel's good will and affection meant more to her right now than just about anything else, especially her immediate surroundings.

"Ooops . . . excuse me," a soft voice broke in, then was gone.

Tearing his lips from the honeyed softness of hers, Daniel chuckled against her hair. "I think that was a hint. You'd better get back to work."

"Mmmmm. Just a minute longer," she whispered, too needful of the reassurance of his heartbeat to move. "If it takes the claustrophobic madness of a supply closet to control you for a minute, I'm not letting go so quick!" It was a mutual holding, with Daniel gently stroking her hair.

"I've got a game tonight, Nia. Can we spend tomorrow together?"

In response to the urgency in his tone, she looked up. "I'd like that," she answered, knowing it was crazy to want to see him, but helpless to resist, then angry at that helplessness. But he was forceful, melting her anger with the warmth of his gaze. She blotted the last of the moisture from her eyes. "I must look awful."

"You look lovely," he crooned with a catch in his voice as he framed her face and kissed her a final time. "Brunch tomorrow—around eleven?"

"No practice?"

"Not until two. If you can find something to occupy you during the afternoon, we can even do something at night."

"Is the practice an open one?" she asked tentatively.

"Yes. . . ." he answered.

"Could I watch?"

"You'd want to do that?" He seemed pleased, and that, in turn, bolstered her.

"I might . . . if you behave yourself during brunch."

"And what is that supposed to mean?" he goaded playfully.

Her smiled faded into an expression that was soft, yet serious. "It means that I don't want to hear any more talk about my writing that article. I'm not doing it! That's a vow! Will you try to trust me?"

The vulnerability she saw when she looked at him blended with his vibrant masculinity to evoke a tugging sensation from deep within her. He held her gaze with magical intensity. For a fleeting instant she wondered whether he had trusted her all along, whether he had goaded her moments earlier because of an inner need in him that was yet to be revealed to her. But then he smiled.

"I think I can do that, babe. If you'll promise to wear old clothes to the practice."

"Old clothes?"

"That's what I said."

"But . . . why?"

"I don't think I can take another round with that lace-necked sweater of yours." He referred to her outfit of that first day; even she had realized that it was out of place. "It's far too distracting." His hands fell from her shoulders to her waist, his thumbs very deliberately brushing the swell of her breasts in the process. "I won't have my team drooling over you. You can save the sexy stuff for me alone. I guarantee you I'll appreciate it."

"Is that a threat?" She grinned, her ego very pleasantly inflated.

"You bet it is," he rasped. "Now let's get out of here before I decide to give you a demonstration. . . ."

seven

NIA HADN'T FELT SO HAPPY IN YEARS. SHE knew it was dumb, that their relationship could go nowhere, yet the knowledge that she'd be seeing Daniel the following day excited her. Her face had a special glow that even the thought of the Mahoney suit could not dull.

In the course of the afternoon—or what was left of it after Daniel left and she had settled back in at her desk—she tackled the usual stream of problems with unlimited patience. Only Priscilla guessed the cause of her newfound lightheartedness, but she said a very diplomatic nothing.

Fate, in the form of a long-standing dinner-and-theater date, precluded any possibility of Nia's watching the game that night. It wasn't until well after the final bell that she bid Barry Riccardi a platonic goodbye on the front porch of her house, then let herself in with a secret smile on her face. It had been a pleasant evening. Barry was a friend, an accountant, a lover of the theater. Yet her thoughts were on the next day.

For over an hour she lay in bed in the dark, eyes open wide. Conjuring up images of Daniel, she wondered what destiny had thrown them together such a surprisingly short time ago. Given her past, he was the *last* man she should have found attractive. But the past *was* past. For the first time, she truly believed it. Had it taken a man like Daniel to exorcise the ghosts? Even the thought of his game was far less odious now.

Ironically, it was precisely that game that she counted on to be her safeguard. It would prohibit the kind of deep involvement she and David had originally thought they could capture and keep. Her relationship with Daniel would be more carefree, more casual, more tentative—and free of all confinement. Daniel would race off on his road trips; she accepted that fully. Indeed, there were no strings whatsoever attached to their friendship. Hadn't she just spent the evening with another man? Granted, she mused, she had refused his offer of a movie date for two weeks hence, but she would surely see him again at some future time.

On an uncharacteristic whim she jumped out of bed and drew a long, hot, bubble-filled bath. It tingled her skin when she first stepped in, its heat sending goose bumps over her. Sinking deeper, she rested her head against the tub's rim and closed her eyes.

It *had* been good talking with him today. There had been the reassurance of discussing a problem with a friend and receiving level-headed encouragement in turn. Had she missed this over the years? Yet she had never thought of herself as a dependent person. On the contrary, willfulness had been more her style. Why, then, was the comfort of knowing Daniel so welcome?

With a hum and a smile amid the wafting steam, Nia pushed all such questions from her mind. The fact remained that he *had* come when she'd needed him and that she *had* appreciated his support. What would happen the next day . . . would happen.

The next day . . . the doorbell rang at ten, a full hour earlier than she had anticipated. Nia was in her robe, reading the newspaper over a final cup of coffee at the tall breakfast bar in the kitchen. A frown creased her sleep-rested features as she went to the front window overlooking the street. A sleek maroon Datsun. How could he do this to her?

"You're early," she exclaimed as she opened the door with an embarrassed grimace. "You said eleven. I just woke up. I haven't showered or dressed."

"So I can see." Daniel smiled, looking her over with enjoyment. "May I come in anyway?"

Nodding, she stepped aside, feeling very self-conscious and just a little naughty as she led the way back upstairs. "Would you like some coffee? You can read the paper while I dress," she called over her shoulder as she sought the sanctity of the kitchen to compose herself.

But Daniel was close behind her, taking in her own half-finished coffee and the open newspaper in a glance. "So this is how you nine-to-five types spend your Saturday mornings?" he teased. At this hour his voice had a deep huskiness that somehow made her all the more aware of her state of undress. Tugging her robe more snugly around her, she mustered a spirited response.

"If I was a nine-to-five type I would spend every morning this way. As it is, I only have the paper delivered on weekends because there isn't enough time during the week to read it and still be in the office by eight-thirty. And, for your information, I rarely leave the office before six or six-thirty. So much for your nine-to-five types!"

He looked unfairly handsome in what seemed to be his uniform—slacks, a blazer and, this morning, an open-necked shirt. There was nothing sleep-mussed or wind-blown about him.

"I don't know, Nia." He shook his head playfully. "With those long lunch hours you people take . . ."

"You were the one who dragged me out to lunch!" she laughed back. "I would have sat at my desk through it all."

"Yeah—you would have brooded there by yourself all afternoon if I hadn't come along."

A deep sigh drew her momentarily straighter. "You're right about that, Dan. I really felt better. Thanks."

Stepping closer before she could anticipate the move, he took her face in his hands. "It was my pleasure," he murmured against her lips, then took them in a gently awakening kiss, the likes of which she would have loved to arise to each and every morning. Like the very first cup of coffee, it was just what she needed to set her senses astir for the day. And, like that very first cup of coffee, rich and robust and hitting the spot, the leisure of the weekend demanded a second.

Nia wound her arms about his neck and leaned more closely against him, offering her lips for the taking. He savored her slowly, draining the warmth of her mouth before nibbling his way down her neck.

"You smell so good." His lips moved against her skin. "Why is that?"

She tilted her head to allow him freer access to the base of her neck and the hollow of her throat. "Lemon-scented bath bubbles," she whispered. "I . . . couldn't fall asleep last night . . ." she gasped as his lips moved lower, ". . . so I took a long and slightly . . . indecent . . . bath. . . ."

Daniel had inched his way back to the bar stool and now lounged against it, his legs outstretched on either side of her. His lips did erotic things to her throat as her fingers clutched his shoulders for balance. She felt strangely dizzy.

"Daniel . . . I'd better . . . get dressed. . . ."

"Indulge me a minute." He spoke thickly, raising his eyes to meet hers for an instant. "You have to admit . . . I've been very . . . good . . . so far. Trust me. . . ."

"I do," she whispered, and he kissed her again, silencing her as his hands gently opened her robe and crept within to touch the silky softness of her body through its sheer, pale gown.

"Do you know that you're beautiful?" he gasped. "Beautiful and sexy?"

"Funny," she moaned in response to the fingers

that traced every curve with maddening slowness, *"I* think *you* are."

"Beautiful?"

"And sexy."

"And how would you know that?" he moaned hoarsely, his breath warm against the upper swell of her breast. "You've never seen me undressed."

Nia clung to his head for support—or was she simply urging him closer? "I don't need to see you undressed to know you're sexy," she chided him, her uneven breathing a sign of the heat he'd loosed within her. "Besides, you've got . . . great . . . hands. They're sexy. . . ."

Those hands began to touch her in earnest, bringing soft whimpers from the back of her throat. "It's where they touch you that's sexy," Dan managed to argue. "Your breasts . . ." His hands cupped them through their silken covering, holding their full weight in his palms as his fingers found each crested tip. "Your hips . . ." His hands fell lower, tracing the cinch of her waist and flaring slightly with her hips before moving behind to the small of her back and pressing her uncompromisingly against him.

"This is . . . getting . . . out of hand . . ." she cried, finding herself wanting him to touch her even more intimately.

"Trust me . . . trust me, babe. . . ." His pleading scratch of a voice was muffled against her skin. "I just need to feel you. . . ."

Her robe slithered to the floor without her even knowing. She was too obsessed by the long, strong fingers, less steady now as they slid beneath the straps of her nightgown and eased its bodice down. Without the support of his steel-banded thighs she might have fallen. But she wanted everything he did to her—her eyes told him so when he looked up in a fleeting question.

She was nude to the waist now, her hands still clutching his shoulders. She watched him as he looked at her, at her body, not touching, simply admiring. Biting her lip, she stifled the plea for his touch, much as she craved it. There was an odd pleasure in watching him watching her, seeing his appreciation of her softly curving femininity in his eyes. He made her feel like an alabaster goddess, worshipping her silently as though almost afraid to touch. . . .

"Aren't you going to . . . ?" she finally whispered, driven by wild fires within.

His tone was choked. "Yes, babe, in time. . . ."

The labored rise and fall of her breasts grew more so when he finally lifted his hands, open palmed, to brush against the rock tautness of her nipples. She trembled and sighed, digging her fingers into the thickness of his hair, following it as it tapered to his nape.

"Daniel . . . Daniel . . ." she half-chided, groaning as he eased the clinging fabric of her nightgown past her navel. His fingers were feather light, sending chills of arousal through her, discovering her flesh inch by precious inch. "Daniel!" she cried, suddenly frightened by the force of her desire, "please . . . stop for me . . . I can't . . . I can't think. . . ."

As he retraced her body upward, her nakedness flamed for him. "It's happened too fast," he whispered, then pulled her against him and held her trembling body so tightly that the intrusive rigidity of his buttons kept her sane.

"I'm not sure I want this," she breathed unevenly, letting her own hands fall to rest on the muscular firmness of his thighs. No, she realized, she didn't want *this.* She wanted him naked, as she nearly was. She wanted to touch every warm inch of him. She wanted to know the beauty of him in the most intimate way. But, of course, she couldn't tell him *that!* Wasn't this to be a casual relationship? Deep physical involvement would spoil all that!

Sensing her fear and feeling some of his own, Daniel slowly held her away from him to replace the nightgown he had so sensually lowered. His jaw was tight with restraint when he stood, set her firmly on her own feet, and stooped to retrieve her robe. It could have been a lush mink coat for the care he took in draping it over her shoulders. Then he bent forward, smoothed the hair from her neck, and put his lips lightly there.

"Go on and get dressed, babe," he mumbled, tonguing her skin in a final erotic way. "There's no rush."

A long, long shower was in order—first cool, then hot—as she pondered his words. As was often the case, she wondered about the double meaning. Was there no rush for brunch—or no rush for lovemaking? In any case, she did take her time, needing the calming period of solitude. She emerged at last feeling pleased, if in a less physical way than when she had fled his arms.

"All set?" he asked, then widened those deep brown eyes of his. "You look great!" His voice was steady and innocently enthusiastic. After draining the last of the coffee to which he'd helped himself during her absence, he carefully folded the newspaper and put it neatly on the counter.

Nia eyed him through her thick dark lashes. "Will I do—for brunch *and* practice?" Much thought had gone into her selection of plum-hued gabardine slacks, a pink blouse and matching sweater.

"You're still up for going?" he asked, giving her a final out.

"Sure! I'm looking forward to it!" And, oddly, she was.

"You know . . ." his voice was lower, ". . . I almost believe you."

"Daniel," she sighed, "I wouldn't say it if I didn't mean it."

"I'm counting on that, babe. I'm counting on that." With a deep breath, he recovered the initiative. "Come on. Let's go."

Brunch was, as she had expected and could appreciate, with the day before's lunch experience under her belt, at a small, very private, quaintly elegant spot in North Cambridge, an easy drive from her house. Daniel managed to go unnoticed by everyone except Nia, whose body simply wouldn't let her forget the lingering sweetness of his touch.

Things were not much better at the practice—but, to her utter astonishment, she loved every minute of it. Every word that Daniel had spoken to her about basketball in the course of their conversations came back to add to her appreciation. The names of the players now had a familiar ring to them—Flagg, Rockowski, Fitzgerald, Jones, Watts, Barnes, Washington. Walker was still out, standing restlessly by the bench, obviously tormented at not being able to play. Other players—backups—were unidentifiable to her; she made a mental note to ask Daniel about them later.

Daniel himself was wearing the team warm-ups, looking handsome as all get-out as he tried to ignore the fact that his very private audience was slouched in her seat, trying her best to look invisible in the fourteenth row up, third seat over, center left.

Nia watched as he directed the practice, calling the plays in that deep timbre she'd come to know so well. She watched as he rounded the players in, demonstrated one point or another, even lashed out with vehemence at the continued mishandling of a particular play. She watched as he turned and conferred with his assistants, then took several minutes out to talk with a gentleman who sat in the shadows several rows up in the stands opposite Nia. Harlan McKay? Again she made a note to ask.

Almost against her will, she found something breathtaking about the demonstration of physical magic on the court. It was at the odd moments—in between practiced plays—that the best occurred, those moments when an individual player would seem to tune out the rest of the world and take off for an intimate rendezvous with the ball.

There was an exquisite rhythm to it, a sense of oneness. Hand and ball were kin, in utter understanding, almost as if connected by a transparent tendon that stretched and retracted in loving communion. At times it seemed that the ball never quite settled down, never quite left the hand, yet wove in and out of endless legs that walked, jogged and ran in succession. It was a dance, a choreographed display of starting, stopping, spinning, darting, slicing fluidly around an imaginary obstacle until, at last, in a soaring thrust, the ball was up and in.

Climactic was the word for it. Nia was grateful for the few minutes it took Dan to shower and dress, for they enabled her to let her appreciation gel.

"What did you think?" he asked, his arm around her shoulders as he walked her toward the car.

"I thought it was . . . impressive," she admitted, downplaying her enthusiasm as a point of pride. Then she grew more sheepish. "Actually, I feel a little guilty. I guess I've unfairly maligned your game just because of what happened between . . . David and me."

"Did it upset you . . . watching?"

"No, doctor," she drawled.

"Not sorry you came?"

"No, doctor." She hesitated then, thinking of David. "Did . . . did *my* presence disturb you?"

"Of course not!" he exclaimed, as though she

were deranged for even suggesting as much. "It was nice to know you were there . . . waiting." The catch in his voice and the corresponding sadness in his eyes seemed to fade as he seated her in the Datsun. She waited for him to slide behind the wheel in that remarkable way he had of tucking his long legs and body into the bucket seat in one smooth, seductive coil.

"Now where?" she asked, taking a deep breath to steady the sudden acceleration of her pulse.

"Shopping."

"Oh? Anything special we're looking for?" Whatever it was, she was game. Having just survived a remarkably pleasant two hours in none other than the arena watching the Breakers in practice, she was up for anything! Perhaps he needed new sneakers. . . .

With a slow purr, the Datsun came to life. Beneath Daniel's sure hand, it glided across the hardtop toward the exit. "I don't know. What do *you* feel like? Better still," he scowled in an expression of endearing bewilderment, "what do you feel like *making?* It's your choice. You're the cook."

"Ahhhh—we're going to the supermarket!"

He grinned. "And where else did you think we might go?"

"Who knows?" she teased him with a pert shrug. "You jock types always seem to need some little doo-hickey or another. You know, shoe laces, sweat bands—"

"Where *do* you pick up your information, Mrs. Phillips?" he cut in, taking mock offense. "I'll have you know that in *our* league the team supplies everything. Do you know that one player's contract even provides him with a Rolls Royce?"

"You're kidding . . . !"

"If only I were! It's getting absurd. Modern players have high-priced sports attorneys who negotiate their contracts. At the end of the negotiations, more often than not, the attorney turns to his client and asks him if there isn't anything, some little something, that he's always wanted but never had. Sometimes it's a lifetime membership in an exclusive golf club, sometimes a house by the lake, sometimes—"

"—a Rolls Royce?"

"Right."

"And what about you, Daniel? Did you ask for any of those things?"

"They weren't offering things like that way back then."

Nia chuckled. "It was only sixteen or seventeen years ago. And your last contracts had to have been negotiated more recently than that. . . ."

"No, Nia. I wasn't interested in that kind of frill. I took as much money as they thought I was worth, lived the modest existence that pleased me, gave my parents whatever I could and invested the rest."

"And . . . ?"

They reached a stop light and he turned to her. His features were calm, solemn. "And, as a result of those investments, I don't have to work another day of my life. That kind of security pleases me, particularly since I've been able to have whatever material pleasures I've wanted as well."

"Could you ever retire?" she asked, wondering how that fine mind could ever stagnate.

"From basketball? Yes. From work of any sort? No."

"What *will* you do . . . when you leave basketball?" She recalled those courses he'd spoken of taking. "Something with your psychology?"

"Perhaps," he stated soberly, then flicked the wheel and turned in at the market. But Nia had felt the stab of the future and it bothered her. No more was said on a personal note until they were back in the car headed in a direction far removed from Cambridge.

Nia put two and two together. "We're going to your place?"

"You sound surprised. If you'd rather not . . . ?"

"No, I'd love that, Dan! It's just that your place is . . . the private you. I wasn't sure you'd ever let me see it."

Reading between the lines, he began to understand her surprise—almost. "I told you yesterday that I won't question you on that again, Nia." He spoke softly and very seriously. "I meant it. I do trust you." Pausing, he grinned. "Besides, I believe you've already penetrated that private world. My house is its least important part."

If the house was "its least important part," it was a very beautiful one nonetheless. As she had guessed, he did live in Weston, about a ten-minute drive from the arena. His neighborhood was a new one, wooded, with an array of homes ranging in style from colonial and split-level ranch to contemporary. Daniel's was of the latter type, set far back from the road and surrounded by a protective shield of pines and maples. Its huge glass panes reflected the verdure, blending the house into the landscape with remarkable success.

"What do you think?" he asked as they stepped from the car.

"I *hate* contemporary houses, but this isn't bad!" she exclaimed with such sincerity that the first part of her statement was quickly forgotten.

Not only was the interior of the house equally impressive, with its heavy reliance on natural wood and living greenery, but the entire afternoon and evening were more enjoyable than Nia could have imagined.

For a while, in the dimming light of day, they walked through the forest of his seemingly endless backyard, talking quietly of small things, personal things, tidbits from their daily lives. Daniel learned that Nia loved cross-country skiing, eating artichokes, and reading travel magazines. Nia, in turn, discovered that Daniel loved canoeing along the Charles River, concerts on the Esplanade and imported ice cream.

Dinner was a collaborative effort that resulted in tender broiled lamb chops, fork-soft baked potatoes and fresh-buttered green beans, complemented from start to finish by the rich bouquet of a fine red wine. The only interruption was a call from Harlan McKay, which Dan quickly terminated. It was after dinner, however, that the real treat came. For it was then that Daniel showed her his den.

It was the most revealing of all the rooms. And it

was the *last* thing she would have expected to find in the home of a professional athlete. But then, Daniel Strahan was no ordinary athlete. She had long since reached that conclusion. Indeed, he was no ordinary man.

The room in question was a masterpiece of rich and sturdy oak, lined with built-in floor-to-ceiling shelves filled with books, journals, research summaries, reprints and magazines—not a one dealing with the game of basketball.

"You're serious about this, aren't you?" she asked, eyeing the large stacks of material on the huge oak desk. Amazement gave her features a bright glow as she perused the room once more. "This isn't exactly the study of a man taking a course in psychology here or there. My God, you've got the psych bulletins for the last ten years, every text I think I've ever seen and then some. Just what is the depth of your interest in all this?" she asked, turning to eye him with deepening suspicion. "Exactly what degree are you working toward?"

He seemed even taller than usual as he gazed down at her. His voice held its typical modesty. "I'm one course plus half a dissertation short of my Ph.D. in Clinical Psychology."

Stunned, Nia could only shake her head in overwhelming admiration. "You're incredible!"

"No, Nia. Not incredible. I'm simply working my way into a profession as millions of postgraduates do every year."

"But you've *got* a profession—"

"A fleeting one, babe, and one that depends far

too much on the body, which ages, and luck. When the body rebels from that daily battering, one coaches. When the luck runs out and the crowd starts to 'boo,' one retires. This," he gestured broadly around the room, "is my retirement. It's my future."

She had a lot to think about that night after Daniel followed every rule of propriety and drove her home, saw her safely into her house and left. There was a depth to the man that commanded her respect. And each reference to the future brought a jitter to her stomach. If only she could pass him off as a simple acquaintance . . . but that was getting harder to do. She'd begun more and more to look forward to seeing him.

He had given her two tickets to Sunday's game after she had confessed to Christopher Daly's loyalty. "Why don't you get him to drive you to the arena. Then you can come with me after the game."

It worked out perfectly. Chris was overjoyed; not only were the seats precious for this, the Breakers' fifty-sixth consecutive home sell-out, but they were four rows behind the Breaker bench. From Nia's standpoint Chris was exactly the friendly face she needed to get her past that final barrier and into attendance at an actual Breakers game. While he cheered his heart out for the home team, Nia was free to watch Daniel, which she did to the exclusion of almost everything else. He was a study in concentration, pacing the sidelines at times, crouching courtside at others, his eye following everything, his expression sober. Wearing a white shirt and muted paisley tie, a navy blazer and light gray slacks, he was a dignified stand-out. Yet he spoke up when inspired, shouting at his men or a referee in that deep, commanding roar of his, pointing emphatically with a minibaton of rolled play diagrams. At regular intervals he would huddle with his team, instructing them in a particular tactic that his observation of the opposition had indicated. When he sent a player back onto the court, it was always with a reassuring pat on the back.

Unfortunately, despite his insightful efforts, the Breakers lost. Later, as Nia waited for him in his office, she prepared herself to console him. What she had expected was depression. What she found was a blend of physical and mental exhaustion. He didn't say much, simply smiled, took her in his arms, and held her for a minute.

"Thanks for being here," he murmured ambiguously, then said no more as they silently drove back to his house. Nia respected his feelings too much to intrude on them until he felt ready to share them. She found pleasure in fixing him steak and eggs while he relaxed on the living room sofa, gazing out at the woodlands beyond. After all, he did so much for her. . . .

"Is it always this way—the losing?" she asked when he finally showed signs of revival.

His smile was sad but resigned. "It's *always* this way. *Period.*"

"Even the *wins?*"

"Even the wins."

"That gruelling emotionally?"

"Every bit," he sighed, shifting on the sofa to take her hand in his. His thumb gently caressed her wrist, pressing lightly against the life that filled her veins. "As the game goes on I can feel my body grow more and more tense. Everything on the outside has to be so controlled. Within, there's always that emotion. I suppose it's part of the excitement, the intensity. Without it I'd feel let down. But it *is* draining." He shot her a crooked grin. "Just give me a minute. I'll be my old self in no time."

Nia knew only the warmth she felt. "I kind of like you this way once in a while," she said, yielding to a spontaneous expression of her thoughts. "It's nice to know that you're human, too."

"Oh, I'm human, all right." His smile grew positively lascivious, leaving no doubt as to his meaning. His actual intent, however, was pure.

They spent the evening in quiet companionship, talking, playing chess, relaxing after the week's stress. The last thing on Nia's mind was the unpleasantness of the pending libel suit against her. She felt delightfully removed from the worries of the world. The phone rang only once—the customary interruption by Harlan McKay—and was fast forgotten.

Daniel's tension, too, disappeared with the passing of the hours. He was loose and easy, a responsive companion. By evening's end he had done nothing more than hold her, occasionally brushing his lips against her hair or cheek. Though her body betrayed her better judgment in its cry for fulfillment, she was grateful for the time he seemed willing to grant her. Things *had* happened quickly. She had barely known Daniel for a week.

In actuality she would have plenty of time to think. The Breakers were leaving on Monday night for the three-game road trip Daniel had already mentioned. Nia had expected it. She knew it was his life—and it was for the best. She'd already been involved in one disastrous sports-oriented relationship. Yet she couldn't help but regret having to say good-bye.

"Here," Daniel said, reaching into his breast pocket to extract a small piece of paper. "I want you to take this. It's our itinerary. Hotel listings where we'll be. Phone numbers. Flight information. If there are any problems here—if anything's troubling you, I want you to call."

Deeply touched by the gesture, Nia didn't know what to say. He was just a friend and she certainly couldn't burden him with her every problem. But he was good for her, getting her to talk things out. Even the Mahoney business, which lingered uncomfortably in the back of her mind, seemed less dreadful when shared with Daniel.

Moved by his thoughtfulness, she swallowed the lump in her throat. "I'm sure . . . everything will be all right. There shouldn't be any—"

He stilled her with a finger on her lips. "Just take it," he whispered. "For my peace of mind?"

As she closed her hand around the paper she knew that he wasn't the only one whose peace of mind would be assured.

eight

TO NIA'S AMAZEMENT, THE WEEK FLEW BY. The rush at work, with her own trip to the Amish country set for the end of the week, was helpful in keeping her mind from the issue of the Mahoney hearing set for the Monday after. Daniel's near nightly calls helped as well. Their talks occurred late, well after the game had ended, Daniel had grabbed something to eat, and returned to his room. He lay in bed as did she, and they shared the day's happenings with an openness that would have startled her if she'd stopped to ponder it. But she didn't. Her future with Daniel was too fragile for analysis, too elusive for comfort. One day at a time. That was all. Daniel never promised to call again. There was never any promise of a day or an hour. But Nia grew excited every time the phone rang, knowing that at that hour it would be him.

Having studied his travel schedule carefully, she

made her own plans accordingly. Flying into Philadelphia early Thursday morning, she spent that day and Friday driving over the countryside west of the city, particularly the region of Lancaster County where the largest Amish colonies existed. By Friday night she was back in Philadelphia and checked into her motel to watch the game between the Breakers and the '76ers in the privacy of her room.

Then the waiting began. She hadn't told Daniel she'd be there, had been purposely vague about the details of her trip when she'd last spoken to him on Wednesday night. There was the fear in the back of her mind that he would be offended, even angry to learn that she had made her own reservations at the same motel in which the Breakers were staying. She had even coordinated her flight back early Saturday morning to mesh with that of the team. He could be furious. Had she done the right thing?

She waited until eleven o'clock, then called Dan's room every ten minutes. It was eleven-thirty before there was finally an answer. As it had each time she'd dialed the extension, her heart raced. Now, at the sound of the deep, familiar, though clearly exhausted voice, it gave an added jump.

"Yes?" The team had won, yet he sounded defeated.

"Dan . . . ?" she began unsurely.

His voice picked up instantly, showering her with pleasure. "Nia! I just called your house! Where are you?"

"Uh . . ." she smiled with timidity at the moment of truth, "would you believe two floors above you?"

"Here? In Phillie?" He *did* sound pleased!

"Uh-huh." Her heart beat even faster.

"But I thought you were flying back to Boston late this afternoon."

"I had originally thought I might. But . . . I changed my mind. I thought it might be kind of fun . . . to be here tonight. I'm flying home tomorrow."

"You did!" he exclaimed as though celebrating a private victory. The smile on his face came clearly over the line.

"Should I . . . could I . . . come down?" This was the hardest part; what did they do now?

"No!" *No?* "Stay there! I'm coming up. What's your room number?"

She had no sooner hung up the phone and wiped the foolish grin from her face than his impatient knock shook the door. The grin reappeared and was returned in kind when she pulled the door open and stood looking at Daniel. He looked great! Tall . . . handsome . . . yes, tired . . . but happy. When he took her into his arms and held her she felt positively complete. Every bit of her anticipatory worry was forgotten amid the beauty of this moment.

"You are a sight for sore eyes," he moaned, kissing her gently, then with mushrooming hunger.

"So are you," she managed to gasp when he finally released her lips.

He kissed her again, compensating for the

week's abstinence. Nia savored the flavor of him, as she always did. His scent was uniquely Daniel, his body likewise. He was her home away from home and she was in no rush to leave. Indeed, had he stripped her naked and made fierce, forceful love to her, she would have clung to him ecstatically.

But he didn't. He was a model of phenomenal self-control. As a coach, he was able to internalize his emotional involvement for the sake of his team, regardless of the effect that rigid control had on him. As a man, his determination was apparently no less strong. For whatever reasons, he had decided against taking his relationship with Nia beyond the point of no return. Now he moved her away from him.

"Let's get out of here, babe, while I still have the willpower. I want to hear all about your trip." He paused, his eyes pouring out his appreciation of her. "God, it's good to see you here!"

The next few hours were spent in a small all-night eatery not far from the motel. It was far from elegant, far from immaculate, far from atmospheric, but there was nowhere else Nia would rather have been and no one else she would rather have been with.

She told Daniel about her sojourn among the Amish folk, those people who believed in separation from the world and neither swore, nor waged war, nor partied in politics. She had seen them working their farms with horses and plows, traveling their roads with horses and buggies. She had been in homes that boasted neither electricity nor telephone lines. She had seen bearded men with their wide-brimmed hats, bonneted women with their plain, long dresses and children who were black-garbed miniatures of their elders. She had spent time talking with those who were willing to open up to her, listening with fascination to their pure, clean, gentle speech. The simplicity of their lives was the antithesis of her own, though she wouldn't have traded with them for the world.

Daniel, in turn, was easily coaxed into talking of the road trip, of a loss in New York, of wins in New Jersey the night before and again that night in Philadelphia. He spoke of the movie he had seen two nights before, of the reading he had done during an idle spell. The latter was an article from a psychology journal which presented the results of a new study on psychosomatic illness. They discussed it at length, with Nia offering her opinions to counter Daniel's more professional ones.

It was nearly three in the morning when Daniel walked her back to her room. There she turned to face him, her eyes offering the silent invitation she couldn't quite speak aloud. Daniel had no such qualms, however, despite the subtle tension in his jaw.

"No, babe. Not yet. You don't really want that kind of involvement any more than I do." He lifted his large fingers to gently stroke her cheek. "This has meant so much to me. Let's be noble for a little while longer."

Nia stared silently at him, knowing that what he said was right, though wondering why he was such a gentleman and half-wishing he were not.

With an unsteady breath, Daniel went on. "I'll call you tomorrow morning to wake you up. Breakfast is at 8:00. OK?"

"You eat as a team?" she whispered with a hint of apprehension, wondering if she were to be suddenly popped on the Breakers . . . or vice versa. Daniel had neither in mind.

"We eat as a team, *you* and *I,"* he qualified in a soft voice. "Any other questions?"

"Just one," she began hesitantly, but had to know. "Are you at all . . . annoyed . . . that I showed up here?" Every aspect of his behavior had indicated the opposite, yet it deeply mattered to her to hear him say so.

In answer he captured her lips a final, punishing time. "Yes," he growled, "I *am* annoyed. I'm going to have an even harder time sleeping alone tonight."

"Then . . . why . . . ?" she burst out before she could help herself.

"Because I don't want to feel guilty afterward," he rejoined, tension and frustration colliding in his blunt response. "And that's all I intend to say on the matter. Now, will you go in and go to bed?"

"Yes, Dan." She smiled and shook her head in admiration. "Good night."

"Good night, babe."

Her reflections soon gave way to sweet dreams of what had been that night and what might have been had Daniel belonged to a different world. Suppose he had a "steady" job, one that allowed him a wife, a home, a family. Suppose he had not been involved with pro basketball—but then he would not be the Daniel Strahan she loved. No, not loved, she assured herself. Liked. Appreciated. Maybe even idolized. But loved? Not again. Not so quickly. And *certainly* not a basketball man! No, she had been through the inferno once; now she was shy of the flames. Daniel was right; *he was right!* Much as she ached for it, physical involvement would only complicate things for them both. And *that* she didn't want, particularly with the deposition-taking around the corner and approaching fast.

True to his word, Daniel woke her from sleep the next morning with a low, husky-voiced hello. They met in the coffee shop for breakfast, then later at the airport, to which Dan had had to travel with his team, if for no other reason than to make sure they all made it. For the first time he was grateful that only the players traveled first class, leaving the coach, assistant coaches, and other team personnel to fly economy. It gave Nia and Dan that much more time together, though the flight to Boston was regrettably brief. Only once was their quiet company broken—by the very man who had the knack of doing just that, Harlan McKay. The team owner accepted an introduction to Nia in a distinctly bothered manner. In turn, Nia's response was instinctively wary.

"Don't mind him," Daniel reassured her when they were alone once again. "I think he's jealous."

"Of *what?*" she clipped back, having been hurt by Harlan's brusqueness.

"Of *you,* babe. I've been putting him off in favor of you lately. It'll take him a little time to adjust, but he'll come around. You'll see." She couldn't quite see, but neither did she care at that moment, for Daniel brushed a light kiss on her lips, making her forget all else. Harlan McKay's scowl as he saw them was missed by them both.

Indeed, Daniel seemed bent on protecting Nia, on keeping her mind averted from any unpleasantness, be it Harlan's strange jealousy or the upcoming deposition. He spent most of the weekend with her, leaving her only to attend a short meeting and practice on Saturday and then, of course, the game against Detroit on Sunday afternoon. During those times Nia worked at his house, not through any reluctance to see either the practice or the game, but rather because of the sheer necessity of doing her own work. Saturday she reviewed the notes she'd taken on her trip, organizing them while they were still fresh in her mind, writing several preliminary passages for her article. Sunday she reviewed the files on the Mahoney case, which she had taken home from the office before she'd left for Pennsylvania. It was imperative that she be sure of her facts, facts concerning the gathering of her background information, the verification of that information, her attempts to personally interview Jimmy Mahoney—to no avail—and the actual writing of the article. Daniel could spare her vexation only so far; beyond that she was on her own. Though he was a marvelous source of both encouragement and distraction, she was tense nonetheless when he finally took her home on Sunday night.

"Everything will be fine," he assured her, imparting his strength to her through his arms, his entire body. "Will you give me a call when it's over? We're playing Golden State tomorrow night, but I should be home until 4:45."

"I'll call," she agreed readily, wishing that he could be by her side during the ordeal. But that was not the nature of their relationship. It was not his responsibility. She was only grateful that he was there on the sidelines, her very good friend who often seemed like so, so much more. . . .

Though she had expected the worst, the deposition was a relatively mild ordeal. It was held in the office of Jimmy Mahoney's personal attorney, with Nia, Bill, Bruce McHale and the counsel for *Eastern Edge* in attendance. It consisted of each of the codefendants being questioned by the plaintiff's attorney, their responses duly recorded by a stenographer. It took no more than two hours. By noon Nia was back at her desk.

"I told you it wouldn't be all that bad," Daniel chided her, having picked up the phone after one short ring.

"It really was surprisingly civil," she returned, amazed that it had been so and much more relaxed now, having heard Daniel's deep voice. "But I hope it wasn't deceptive. He could really lash out now. You can never tell with these political animals."

"Come on, Antonia, don't ask for trouble. For all you know it might fade into nothing. It's always possible that, having taken your deposition, his attorney will advise against the proceedings. After all, there was no malice of intent."

"*I* know that and *you* know that, but Jimmy Mahoney may try to prove otherwise."

"Well," he sighed, "there's no point in worrying about that now. Austen and McHale are right in there with you. They'll let you know what's happening." He paused. "Are you still planning to go to Vermont tomorrow?"

With a deep breath, Nia allowed the shift of subject. "Yup. Reiss is expecting me by eleven. I've already done some of the preliminary research on him, and I'll do a little more this afternoon. With a three-hour drive each way, I'm not eager to make the trip more than once if I can help it."

"You're sure you don't mind the driving? I don't like the idea of you alone in a car for six hours."

"Look at it this way," she teased him softly, "if I'm alone I can't get into any trouble."

"Nia, you know what I'm talking about."

"I know, Dan. And, believe me, I do appreciate it." It had been a long time since anyone had worried about her. But as gratifying as the thought was, it was also frightening. To grow dependent on such concern only to have it withdrawn . . . Her eyes clouded momentarily, then cleared. "I'll be OK. I've got towing coverage in case the car gives me any trouble. And the trip will be broken up for those few hours in the middle."

"You'll come directly here on the way back?"

They had already discussed the possibility, though at the time Nia had only said she'd consider it.

"I will," she agreed, knowing she was getting in deeper but unable to stop herself. She was already looking forward to seeing him. Tomorrow evening seemed like such a long way off. "I may not be there until six. Is that OK?"

"I'll be here," he growled in mock scolding.

Not only was he there when she returned, slightly exhausted, from her interview with Thomas Reiss on Tuesday, but he was at her office to take her to lunch on Wednesday, and there again on Thursday evening to pick her up from work. They seemed to be very comfortably falling into a pattern that worked around both their schedules. When he had an evening game they met for lunch; when his evening was free, they had dinner and spent the hours together.

For Nia these days and evenings were filled with warmth and pleasure. Her time away from Daniel seemed to fly because of the knowledge that she would be seeing him soon. The only damper on her pleasure was the purely physical strain she had begun to feel. Daniel had become her closest friend; gradually, that ceased to be enough. In utter contradiction to everything she had thought she believed such a few short weeks ago, she wanted to be with him constantly, as a friend *and,* she finally admitted to herself, as a lover.

Her thoughts were filled with him—his lean length, his dark good looks, his thoroughly masculine aura. She dreamed of him at night, imagining the solid feel of his flesh beside hers, yearning for the richness of him even more intimately. She day-dreamed of him at work, feeling foolish when her cheeks grew warm and her pulse raced, ostensibly over some dry piece she had been assigned to edit.

If Daniel suffered similar frustrations she didn't

know it. He insisted on returning her home each night with a kiss—sometimes soft, sometimes more fierce, sometimes nearly explosive with passion—but it went no further. In her heart Nia knew something had to give. It was a hopeless situation, one doomed by incompatible lifestyles. Fool that she was, she *did* love him. And she knew of only one additional way to express that love—and *he* seemed dead set against it.

It was in light of her newly emergent feelings that her trip to Connecticut on Friday was positively tedious. Oh, it was an easy two-hour drive to Hartford and the interview with the Honorable Jonathan Trent went as smoothly as she might have hoped. He was a pleasantly charming, good-looking man—but she found that she couldn't muster up an ounce of personal interest. Her thoughts were all on Daniel. She spent four hours—two each way—brooding on what was to come of their relationship. She wanted to be with him constantly. Hers was an emotional hunger that seemed insatiable. How could she handle this? How could she continue to spend this time with Daniel on a purely platonic level? Granted, there were those kisses, the occasional deeper embrace, even a momentary loss of control—until Daniel regained equilibrium again. Always Daniel. Perhaps his feelings for her were quite different from hers for him. Perhaps they weren't even half as deep. Hadn't he once said that he didn't want to feel guilty after making love to her? That seemed to imply a fear of "using" her. Evidently he was far from being in love himself.

When Nia drove up his long drive on Friday evening and let herself into his house with the key he had given her the night before, she had no way of anticipating what was to come. He was at the arena now; she would watch the game on his television set, then wait for his return.

With a luxury that his presence would not have afforded, she wandered from room to room. Its openness gave her a sense of freedom, even as its every niche was crammed with Daniel. She recalled him as he'd sat one day at his desk, a vee-neck sweater over his bare chest, his sleeves pushed up to his elbows. She had touched that vee with its warm mat of hair and had traced the tendons of those forearms. She wandered to his bedroom, *his bedroom,* with its velour-covered oversized bed, and conjured up images of him sprawled atop it—dressed, partially dressed, then finally with nothing at all as cover save that with which he had been born.

How could she have fallen in love after all that she'd been through once? But as many times as she asked herself the question, the fact remained that she did love Daniel. He affected every aspect of her life and she found herself affected by every aspect of *his.*

He, too, had been more tense of late. With the end of the regular season only two-and-a-half weeks away it was inevitable that he should brood about its outcome. The Breakers had just about clinched their playoff spot; another two wins would do it. It seemed inevitable—yet he had every right to uneasiness. Granted, there was money at stake. More importantly, there was his job. And, of course, there was his pride—and the joy he derived from the game. She had never been able to deny that—she never would. Indeed, she couldn't even deny the pleasure *she* felt at *his* joy—be it in basketball or anything else in life.

With this blunt reminder she helped herself to a snack and switched on the game to watch the Breakers soundly defeat the Bucks for one of those two crucial wins. The jubilation on the floor and from the broadcasting booth was shared by Nia—the very last thing she would have expected to feel three weeks ago. Then she would never have been interested even in the fact of the win, much less have watched its accomplishment with wide violet eyes. How things had changed!

By the time Daniel returned Nia had prepared a feast to honor both the victory and the victor who had engineered it. She had no way of knowing that Daniel's pleasure was only in part related to the win, that her presence in his home had made that win nearly incidental to the delight of returning to a brightly lit place brimming with the warm scent of veal parmesan à la Antonia.

She had never done this for him before—waited at his house, fixed him a late meal. During the week, with each early morning in the offing, it was too impractical to consider driving back to Cambridge at such a late hour. This was Friday night, however, and playing house was as much a genuine treat as it was a novelty.

Despite Nia's protestations that she could drive herself, Daniel insisted that she leave her car at his house and returned her to Cambridge himself. It was one-thirty. The hours had flown by amid gentle talk and shared thoughts. He had promised to pick her up for breakfast—a final breakfast before the team left for its six-game stint on the West Coast. That, in itself, was a subtle form of tension, an anticipated loneliness. It was also, however, a stark reminder to Nia of the importance of keeping that last physical barrier in place, much as she abhorred it more as each moment together passed. Once they became lovers—*if* they became lovers—these separations would be devastating. Hers was the voice of experience.

The silence between them was particularly tangible that night as they rounded Soldier's Field Road and the Harvard Stadium to cross over the Longfellow Bridge into Harvard Square. It was the more scenic route he had chosen, as though he, too, was prolonging their time together. They sailed easily through the square and on down Brattle Street, finally turning in at Nia's street. Signs of distress were everywhere.

"My God, there's a fire!" she exclaimed, wondering which of her unfortunate neighbors had been hit. The end of the road—her end—was a confusion of red lights and blinkers, totally blocked off by fire engines and police cars, making it necessary for Daniel to park at a distance. Nia jumped from the car to be hit by the acrid smell of burning that permeated the air. There was no sign of either flame or smoke, though; whatever the problem, it was apparently under control.

Daniel was right beside her, taking her hand.

"Let's take a look. If there's been a fire at the house next to yours I don't know if I like the idea of you—"

"Daniel!" she shrieked, at last seeing the object of the firemen's powerful floodlights. "It's mine! Oh, my God . . . !"

"Come on." He tightened his grip. "We'll see what's happened."

Less than an hour later they were headed back toward Weston, barely able to assimilate what they had seen and learned through conversations with the firemen. As Nia shook her head slowly the passing street lights lent a flickering sheen to her hair. "Thank goodness he's all right!" she cried shakily. "Material loss is one thing. If Dr. Max had been hurt it would have been so much more horrible. As it is . . ." Her voice trailed off in dismay.

Daniel kept the car at a steady clip. "Fortunately he woke up in time and had the presence of mind to get out of the house. At his age he could well have become disoriented. It's a miracle that the flames hadn't spread to the front room where he'd fallen asleep. The entire back of the house was involved before he woke up." He sighed. "According to what the fireman said, he feels guilty as hell. . . ."

"Pipe ash," she half-sobbed. "I never even knew he smoked a pipe."

"From what his daughter told them, he never did. Not regularly, at least. He had an old collection of them. Must have decided to have a smoke on some kind of crotchety old whim. When he didn't care for the taste he knocked the ash into the wastebasket. That's all it takes—a few tiny bits of glowing tobacco and a basket full of crumpled paper. It was slow to start, but once it caught, it went!"

Nia gave a low moan of helplessness, then began to tremble uncontrollably. As if his words had not been vivid enough, the smell of destruction clung to her clothes and, even more bitterly, her memory.

"Everything, Dan. Everything's ruined!" she cried in abject misery. "What am I going to do?" It was an overwhelming thought, that of rebuilding from scratch.

"For starters, babe, you're going to keep calm and cool." His voice, as if in example, was level and reassuring, its tranquilizing effort enhanced by the sure hand that encompassed hers and brought it to rest on his thigh. "You're going to stay at my place—"

"Daniel, I can't do that!"

"You can. And you will. Tomorrow—er, today—we'll go out and get you some clothes to wear. Monday morning you can talk with your insurance company. Little by little you can replace what you've lost."

"I can't believe this! Any of it!" Despite what he had said and his deliberate attempts to calm her, she felt near hysteria. Nothing like this had ever happened to her—this sudden, completely unexpected, utterly total loss. "I've got nothing left but the clothes on my back. The house . . . it was home for more than ten years. . . ."

"I know, babe. I know." He brought her hand to

his lips and breathed his warmth onto her chilly skin. "Everything will work out. Believe me, it will."

But she wondered. The prospect of the immediate future suddenly terrified her. She felt lost, uprooted, floundering in an instant limbo. If she had felt any numbness at the scene of the fire, the last of it had worn off by the time they reached Daniel's house. He insisted that she sit down while he poured her a snifter of brandy, then sat with her to make sure she drank it all. It helped, steadying her some, easing the queasiness she'd felt in the pit of her stomach.

"I still can't believe this," she repeated in a whisper, shaking her head, burying her face in her hands.

Reaching for her, Daniel drew her against his strength, holding her with arms that were steady and sure. "It'll take a while, Nia. It's understandable that you should feel in shock."

"That's an understatement," she breathed against his chest, inhaling the richness of his manly scent as a counterpoint to that other, harrowing one. "Do you think that anything will be salvageable?"

"I don't know, babe." He absently stroked her upper arm, rustling the silk of her blouse against her skin. "The fire reached the roof at the back of the house. I doubt there's much worth saving there. As for the front, what wasn't touched by flame is probably damaged by either smoke or water." Tucking in his chin to look down at her, he grew more stern. "I don't want you going over again . . . until I get back."

Nia met his gaze in disbelief. "But you'll be gone for nearly ten days! I've *got* to go—"

"No, you don't. I have a friend. Actually, Peter is the brother-in-law of our trainer, Hickey Simms. Peter is a handyman-carpenter of sorts . . . and he has a truck. I'll call him later and *he'll* go to the house. I trust him to remove anything that's worth saving or fixing. You let the insurance adjuster go there by himself. When I get back I'll take you over—it's far too upsetting for you and there's absolutely nothing you can accomplish by going there at this stage. Insurance claims take time, as does the emotional healing from this kind of upset."

Overcome by sudden lethargy, Nia couldn't argue. Daniel had taken over and she was half-glad to let him do so. The thought of her house, now a mass of charred ruins, sent a chill through her that even the brandy could barely control. Daniel was right. The mess they had seen tonight had been obscured by the dark; in the harsh light of day it would be that much more traumatic for her. Perhaps she did need time to gradually accept the reality of it all.

"Come on, babe." He coaxed her to her feet, having studied her despairing expression long enough to convince him that she needed something, preferably rest. "I think you ought to go to bed—"

"—I don't think I can sleep."

"You can try." As he talked he led her down the hall, past his own bedroom to the guest room just beyond. "The bed is already made up." His deft hand flicked back the coverlet. "Wait here. I'll get something for you to wear." In an instant during which Nia did not so much as blink, he was gone and back, bearing what was obviously the top to a pair of navy blue pajamas. "The bathroom's got towels; there are extras in the vanity below the sink." He held her gaze with a tenderness, born of worry, that touched her even through her silent anguish. "Why don't you take a long, hot shower?" He smiled. "It will help you relax."

"Maybe I will," she whispered, her eyes infinitely sad. "And . . . Daniel . . . ?"

"Yes?"

"Thanks . . ."

"For what?"

"For . . . being here. For . . . taking charge . . . helping me."

In the wake of her soulful expression a fierceness flashed across his features, his torment comparable to hers.

Shoulders bowed beneath his own burden, he stepped back. "I'm . . . glad I was here," he murmured, then turned and with a raspy "good night" left the room, pulling the door firmly shut behind him.

Given the events of the evening, Nia was unable to focus on the long-range implications of Daniel's frustration. Visions of smoke and flame permeated her mind. And neither the brandy nor Daniel's valiant attempts at encouragement was able to stem her stubbornly self-renewing sense of shock. She felt totally helpless, empty and alone. More than anything, she wished that Daniel would have stayed with her. But . . . that was absurd! He was simply next door!

Following his suggestion, she stripped and doused herself beneath the restorative spray of the shower, washing away the imaginary grime left by the destruction of her home. The cleansing of her body was, however, a simple matter compared to that of her mind. The vision of her past, her security, her home, was suddenly and irreversibly marred.

Her feet left faint imprints on the plush pile of the almond-colored carpet as she walked back into the bedroom wearing nothing but Daniel's pajama top. With rolled-up sleeves and falling to mid-thigh, it would have been an adequate night shirt had it not been for the image it conjured up of another body filling it. Frustrated, she stood before the mirror to comb her fingers through the layers of her hair, pushing it here, then there, then frowning in dissatisfaction.

A soft oath escaped her as she threw herself on the bed to lie there for no more than a minute before she bolted up again. Her body was cool, yet it flamed. Her mind was a mass of grief overshadowed by a need that grew greater and greater. She paced the floor. She stopped. She slumped into a chair. She stood up. She thrust her fingers through her hair, then hung her head and paced some more. Finally she came to an abrupt halt.

Her material past had been wiped out. Was it symbolic? Damn it, *she needed him.* Was she wrong to fight the welling ache? She desired him. She *loved* him. Was it wrong to go to him? But he had been the one to stop short in the past. Would he turn her away again?

Debate was pointless. Her need had far exceeded the value of hashing and rehashing what was right or wrong. Nia only knew that at this moment she could not stay in this room, alone. Daniel was her only hope.

Driven by a determination stronger than any she'd ever felt, she whirled and headed for the door, drawing it quickly open and entering the hall. Daniel's door was open; his light was on. But he was nowhere in sight.

Her heart beat madly as she followed the hall toward the living room. There, silhouetted against the glass, he stood, his back to her, his hands on his hips, his head bowed with emotion. Whether it was anger, frustration, sadness, or simply exhaustion she didn't know. And there was only one way to find out.

On silent feet she approached, fighting against the incipient trembling that his appearance had sparked. He was a lean mountain of gleaming flesh, bare skin from shoulder to hip and then again from thigh to toe. He wore nothing but a dark pair of shorts, the bottoms to her tops, if her guess was correct. The dampness of his body suggested that he, too, had just emerged from a shower. He was, even in the darkness, every bit as magnificent a male creature as she had imagined him to be.

"Daniel?" she whispered from just behind him.

His head turned toward her, a damp swathe of hair falling across his brow. Then he looked away. "What are you doing, Nia?" He was angry.

"I need you, Dan."

He gritted his teeth. "Damn it, Nia. You'll only be hurt!"

"I've already been hurt. Now I need *you.*" Her hand wavered in the air close to his back. His body warmth lured her palm and she lowered it, touching the firmness of his flesh. It was all she could do not to cry out at its beckoning strength.

Daniel stiffened for an instant, shooting her another sidelong glance. His eyes reflected the moonlight; they held more vehemence now than anger. "I have to leave today. Do you know what that means? I can't be with you. I can't be here when you need me. Is that what you want?"

"I want you . . . now."

"But what about tomorrow? And the next day . . . or week . . . or month? You've been through this, Nia. I can't promise you anything!"

Closing her eyes, she moved against his back, wrapping her arms around his rock-hard middle and laying her cheek against his skin. Its vibrancy enhanced her own determination. Nothing he could say would change her mind.

"I hear everything you're saying, Dan, but I need you." She tightened her arms about him, spreading her fingers over his ribs. "I want you. Please . . . please don't send me away." There was no pleading in her voice, simply an expression from the heart. Responding to it, he turned in her arms, looking down at her with far greater tenderness.

"Do you have any idea how hard it's been for me to turn away from you time and again? Do you have any idea what I want, babe?"

"Is it all that different from my need, Dan?" she asked, her eyes filled with the ache that she felt so deeply.

He seemed to grow more fierce before her eyes. "No, perhaps it isn't. It's every bit as demanding and all-consuming. *And* every bit as futile." His tone softened. "Don't you see, babe," he murmured sadly, "I didn't ask for you, either! I didn't ask for this wanting and needing. And I don't know what in the hell to do about it!"

Nia ran her hands through the matted coarseness on his chest and felt the warm, pulsing beat of his heart. "Can't we just have now, this minute, this simple beauty, regardless of any future?" His texture fascinated her, capturing her gaze. She breathlessly admired the endless expanse of flesh, its well-formed muscle, its strategically placed furring. Driven by a burning deep within, she leaned against him and put her lips to that heated plain. His arms closed instinctively behind her.

"Oh, babe," he rasped out his agony, "I do want you."

"Then take me!" she cried, desperate at last. *"Do it!"*

With a force as close to violence as he had ever come, he gripped her face in the vise of his hands and forced it upward. His eyes pierced hers in the darkness, surging into her trembling soul, searching for the answer to his anguish. It was there.

With a moan of surrender he crushed her lips beneath his, yielding to a pent-up hunger that devoured with the ferocity of that initial burst of released desire. She barely had time to gasp for air when he swept her off her feet and into his arms, cradling her protectively as he strode down the hall to the room with the low light, his room.

As though the first flurry of emotion had relieved him of that utter urgency, he laid her down amid the disarray of his sheets with a renewed gentleness. There was an animal sensuality about him as he slowly stretched out against her on the bed. Nia gasped at the beauty of his body, exploring the sturdiness of his arms and shoulders, the swell of his chest, as she had never had the freedom to do before.

He kissed her more tenderly then, parting her lips for the sweeping invasion of his tongue. Nia met it and offered it her essence, winding her own around it in an instinctive dance that was only the start of the mating she craved. She arched toward him, needing far more than his kiss, feeling his greater need, hard and strong against her. In that instant, wanting to give him everything, she deeply resented the night shirt he had so gallantly given her earlier.

They were well attuned to one another. Reading her thoughts, Daniel sat up, panting, and steadied himself as he drank of the passion-glow in her cheeks. Her eyes held the undisguised, sweet violet joy of anticipation that expressed far more than the rapid rise and fall of her chest.

Nia waited, watched, silently loved him with every fiber of her being until he finally moved his hand to the top button of her shirt and released it. There was a second, then a third, each widening, lengthening that strip of ivory flesh, his to adore.

She had never remembered wanting a man like this, had never remembered needing to be touched so badly. The years had given her a maturity that added to every ounce of her appreciation.

With the final button Daniel pushed the dark fabric aside. His hands trembled under the strain of control, the effort toward a leisure that denied the thrust of his own aching need. She felt the cool air for an instant until the fire of his gaze began its descent, warming her throat, each breast in turn, her middle, her legs, the completeness of her naked beauty.

"Oh, Nia . . ." He barely managed a scratching whisper as his hands traced the journey his eyes had just completed. "Nia . . ."

As ever, her level of self-control was much lower than his. In his presence she forgot all else. There was neither her work nor his nor that nightmare of destruction they had both witnessed earlier. There was only Daniel, in the firm, virile flesh, moving toward her.

"Daniel," she moaned, and when his fingers found her, she arched herself against them in dire need. "It seems that I've wanted you so very long," she begged raggedly. "Please . . . hurry. . . ."

He moved back, then straightened and skimmed her cream-soft length again. His eyes smoldered with the deep fires of yearning that this woman had lit in him; he, too, had waited forever. With slow deliberation he dropped his hands to his waistband and lowered his shorts.

The male perfection of him was nearly more than Nia could bear. He was an athlete from top to bottom, leanly masculine, vibrantly hard. Courting warnings of imminent explosion, she scrambled to kneel on the bed before him. There was so much to touch—he was so supremely, masculinely beautiful.

And she did touch him, stroking the lines of his body, caressing the sensitive points that he couldn't deny. At last she knew the full measure of the power that she held over him.

"So strong and beautiful," she murmured, drunk with passion as she stretched upward toward him. Her arms circled his neck to bring their bodies flush against one another. His nakedness incited her ardor as hers did his; she was scarcely aware that he had slipped the shirt from her shoulders until his hands spread across her bare back and bottom, pressing her ever closer. It was with an unconsciously fluid grace that this tall man's frame followed her back to the bed. Their bodies meshed instinctively, his long, lean, rangy one settling over her, his hips fitting snugly between her thighs. Simultaneously they had reached the limit of control.

"Now, Daniel, now . . ."

"Yes, babe . . ." Then he cried aloud, a fevered cry of victorious possession as he claimed what her love offered.

For Nia there had never been anything quite so rich as the sharing which she had with Daniel. He was brilliant in his pace setting, positively masterful in his reading of her body. Had he loved her with all his heart—as she did him—he could not have worshipped her more. In turn, he responded to her knowing fingers with a height of arousal that lifted them both far beyond anything either of them had known in the past.

Later, snuggling exhausted in Daniel's protective embrace, Nia marvelled at the rarity of their joint explosion and wondered why life couldn't always be so glorious.

"Daniel . . . ?" she whispered, tipping her mahogany head back to study him. "Dan . . . ?" His eyes were closed, their dark lashes lying luxuriously above his cheekbones. There was a light sheen of perspiration on his forehead and nose, a similar dampness on his chest.

"Ummmm?" One dark brown eye opened, warm still in the aftermath of their loving.

Suddenly Nia didn't know what to say. What she *wanted* to say was "I love you," yet she couldn't permit herself that luxury. It would only complicate things. It would only make things worse. There was still the light of day with which to contend . . . and the utter futility of her love. It was best that it was left unpledged.

Lowering her lips, she feather-touched them to the flat dot of his nipple. His helpless gasp was emotionally satisfying. "Are you . . . all right?" she asked softly.

"Better than all right." He smiled, lifting a hand to caress her face. "That was the nicest thing that's happened to me in a very, very long time."

"Me, too." She hesitated. "You're not sorry?"

He spoke so gently that his words brought tears

to her eyes. "Of course I'm sorry, babe. I'm sorry that I can't spend the next four weeks here in bed with you."

"Coming from you," she smiled, "that's quite a compliment. The next four weeks are the height of your season."

"Not anymore."

"No?"

"No!" He grinned wickedly. With a firm but gentle hand he pulled her atop him. "There . . ." He drew out the word in a long sigh of relief at their renewing intimacy. "This beats all. . . ." Then, with a thorough kiss that stirred her senses afresh, he gave her a second very graphic, very powerful demonstration. She had no further argument.

Unfortunately, Harlan McKay did.

nine

IT WAS THE SOUND OF DANIEL'S ANGRY VOICE that first pierced her consciousness. Confused and groggy, she sat up, struggling to recall where she was and why. Her tousled head swung toward the open door when his deep voice thundered again.

"I know that, Harlan, but the team can just do without me for a few hours. For God's sake, I'll be there tomorrow morning!" There was a pause for the Breaker owner's argument. Then Daniel spoke again, his voice taut. "I know what my contract says, and this *is* an emergency. You supposedly pay assistant coaches to cover for me at times like these." Again a pause. "Damn it, Harlan, I am not *abandoning* you! Something personal has come up; I've already changed my reservations to an early morning flight out tomorrow. With the time change, I'll be in San Diego well before the game." Pause. "That's my business," more sternly, "not yours." Pause. "Harlan, don't be ridiculous! If it's team morale you're worried about, you can tell them I've got the flu and didn't want to infect any of them. I can assure you they'll never miss me." A final pause and a sigh. "I'll *be* there. Ten A.M. their time. Good-bye, Harlan."

Nia barely had time to pull the sheet over her before Daniel appeared at the door. He wore nothing but a thick terry towel slung low on his hips. His hair was wet and mussed. It was obvious that she had slept through his shower as well as at least one other phone call.

When he saw that she was awake his scowl melted instantly. "Hi, babe." He smiled gently. "I'm sorry. Did that wake you?"

Returning his smile, she held out her hand and drew him down to sit beside her on the bed. "It's all right. I wouldn't have wanted to sleep had I known you were up."

"You didn't get much sleep," he chided, arching a dark brow suggestively.

"As I recall," she mirrored the look, "neither did you." Then she recalled the urgency of the situation and sobered. "Daniel, you didn't have to change your plans—"

"I wanted to."

"But I don't expect you to do things like that. You've got to leave with the team. I know that. I've known it all along." Which didn't make the prospect any more appealing, of course.

With a lunge that she didn't expect Daniel took her hands, held them apart and pinned her to the bed. His body loomed above her and he had a look of good-humored determination. "Look, Antonia," he drawled her name with gusto. "I've just informed Harlan that I will be taking a later plane. The arrangements have already been made. My reservations have already been changed. Everything is done. And I haven't done anything but what *I wanted to do!* Now," he took an exaggerated breath, "I've had my fill of back-talk for the morning. Are you ready to go shopping?"

Her heart brimming with a happiness that spilled onto her cheeks in a rosy blush, she shook her head.

"No?" He eyed her, skeptical of the mischievous grin that played across her lips. Again she shook her head.

"And why not?" The corner of his mouth twitched when she shrugged. Releasing her hands, he reached for the sheet that covered her. He had obviously begun to understand. Her hands free to touch him now, Nia made that understanding complete. It was some time before they were, in fact, ready to go.

It was less than twenty-four hours later that Nia stood at the window of the airline terminal watching Daniel's plane pull away from the boarding tunnel, turn, and slowly taxi toward the runway. The pale pink light of day was fast warming to yellow as it spilled glowingly over Boston Harbor.

It was barely seven in the morning. They had been up since five. But then, sleep had not been a major priority in either of their minds since Friday. Their time together had been far too precious to be wasted.

Nia braced her hand against the thickness of the window as the plane moved further off. Daniel had been wonderful. Patient. Compassionate. Fun. Even loving, if she gave way to her own wildest imaginings.

They had spent most of Saturday shopping—for a new head-to-toe and down-to-the-skin wardrobe for Nia, for a full supply of food for her stay at his house, even for a few things that *he* needed for the trip to the West Coast. There had been time to talk, and time to walk in the woods, and, of course, time to make love.

The now-distant plane disappeared for several moments, then reappeared in a whirr of motion—or was it the misting of her eyes that blurred it so?—as it crossed her line of vision, surging faster and further, then off and up, higher into the sky and away. He was gone.

Nia took a deep breath, only then growing aware of the racing of her pulse that had accompanied the plane's ascent. It had taken a part of her with it; she would surely need time to adjust. In the past day she had come to love him more than ever, and it hurt, this parting. A long ten days would pass before she saw him again. Already she missed him!

Without him the house would be lonely, though signs of him were everywhere. Was that part of the punishment—to be so near yet so very far away? Tonight she would sleep in his bed, feeling lost in its bigness, cool without his warmth. Her mind would recreate the solid feel of him against her, the musky scent of his skin on the sheets, the even cadence of his breathing by her ear. And his passion—that would be pure memory.

With a soft groan she turned her back on the window and headed for the car. The past thirty-six hours had been the most beautiful she had ever known, remarkably so considering the harrowing nature of the turn of events that had thrust them together Friday night. But it was the beauty that stood out, the joy, the love; she was convinced that to have lived these hours was worth the agony she might well suffer now.

Her first order of business Monday morning was a stop at Bill Austen's office to tell him what had happened to her house on Friday night. She would be staying with a friend, she told him, then handed him the number in case he needed to contact her after hours.

He recognized the phone exchange instantly. "Weston? A friend?"

"That's right," she answered awkwardly, hoping she had imagined the suspicion in his voice. "He's away. I'm keeping his house company."

Had it been her inability to look him straight in the eye that had given her away . . . or the quiver in her voice . . . or the one clue she'd inadvertently dropped? Whatever it had been, Bill guessed accurately. "Strahan?"

"He's away."

"But it *is* his house?"

"Yes." Thank goodness she had long since told Bill that Daniel was out of the feature. A replacement had even been found in one Chad Donnelly of Atlanta, the country's top seeded racquetball player.

A sly smile—a rarity for Bill—added to her chagrin, however. "I was wondering whether that relationship would go anywhere."

"Bill, that's a truly presumptuous thing to say."

"No, Nia. Simply observant. And certainly not meant as any kind of an insult. From what the men around here say, you're damned fussy about who you see. And from the little I know about Strahan, you could have done worse."

"He's a fine man!" she burst out in defense.

"*I* know that. Wasn't *I* the one who recommended him for this story in the first place?"

Nia blushed. "You were."

"And your opinion of the man now is quite a turnaround from the blatant skepticism I heard in this very office just about a month ago," he teased her lightly. Only later would it occur to her that he, too, was trying to help her forget about the ruin of the house. Right now, she was embarrassed.

"We all make mistakes."

"I'm glad you can admit it."

"And speaking of admitting errors," she deliberately changed the subject while she had a modicum of poise left, "has there been any further word from Mahoney?"

Bill shook his head. "We don't really expect any. He got his publicity with the deposition. Our lawyers feel that he won't push his luck by blowing it out of proportion. It could backfire on him." Nia snorted her disgust but Bill went quickly on. "Don't worry about things here. We're all together on this Mahoney thing and the magazine—every publication in the city, for that matter—is behind us all the way. As far as the house goes, if you've got to take care of cleaning up, we'll cover for you. You've been doing more than your share for months."

Relieved by his support and appreciative of his offer, she smiled warmly, "Thanks, Bill. I've got to contact the insurance company and make a few other calls, but I probably won't do much else until Daniel—" The spontaneous confession had slipped out unbidden; Nia bit her tongue.

But Bill rose to the occasion with instant reassurance. "It's all right. I'm glad he's there to help you." He tucked his chin lower and peered over the rim of his glasses. "Is it very difficult . . . his traveling? I know how you feel about that sport."

There was a sadness to her chuckle that was echoed in her wide violet eyes. "You do, don't you." She sighed in resignation. "Yes, it is difficult. There are those of us in life, I'm afraid, who are simply gluttons for punishment."

"The team is on the West Coast, isn't it?" he asked, frowning. "Uh-huh. For ten days. Uh—make that nine. You see," she forced a brightness as she directed her encouragement inward, "the time does pass!"

Very, very slowly. With a wealth of loneliness. And more than a smattering of doubt. What a fool she had been to fall in love! And with this man! Insane! She had known precisely what to expect; there was no one to blame but herself. To compound the misery she was staying at his house—granted, under extenuating circumstances, but staying at his house nonetheless. What kind of an idiot was she? If she possessed any common sense she would be out looking for an apartment in which to stay until the house was rebuilt . . . or the land sold. The future was in such doubt—perhaps that was why she stubbornly clung to Daniel. He was a steadying force, a friend, and regardless of what became of their affair, she somehow knew she could count on him.

He called her once a day and his voice was instantly reviving. The road trip had begun with jet lag and a particularly frustrating loss to San Diego on Sunday. No, Harlan was not still angry at him. Yes, he was managing to slowly catch up on his sleep. And . . . he missed her. Why, *why* did he say things like that? It only made hanging up that much more difficult!

It was during the interminable stretches between calls that Nia agonized. Against her will she recalled the long separations from David—separations during which, she was later to learn, he had had himself one hell of a good time. Was Daniel doing the same now? There was always that doubt, that nagging doubt. It was simply a question of how long she could bear it.

The second game of the trip was played on Tuesday night against the Phoenix Suns. With a decisive Breaker win, the division title was clinched for the New England team. Daniel's relief was contagious; he was much more relaxed when he called her, and she, in turn, was pleased. But he had awakened her from a nightmare of loneliness and betrayal when he'd called at a very late one in the morning, eastern time. At the end of the game she had promptly dozed off, having decided that he wouldn't call. Now, not more than twenty minutes later, she awoke with a jerk. Even in her hazy state, his affection and honest-to-goodness excitement flowed clearly over the line. The connection was no sooner severed, however, than she grew fearful again. Was he out on the town now, enjoying that carefree bachelor existence? It was his by rights, yet the thought of his holding another woman as he had held her hurt.

Misery kept her up for much of the night and she was less than her cheerful self, indeed, downright grumpy, when she reached the *Eastern Edge* stronghold the next morning. While stalled in a messy traffic jam at the turnpike exit she had vowed to wait until Daniel returned, then move out and away, lock, stock and barrel. She was still her own boss, she had informed herself with an indignant and thoroughly self-reproachful scowl!

Yet when Bill appeared at her office with a long envelope that just happened to contain the specifics of a *Western Edge* assignment and a series of plane tickets that would take her into Los Angeles on Thursday, then on to San Francisco on Friday through the following Tuesday night, she was positively ecstatic.

"Bill! How did you ever manage it?"

"I managed," was all he would say, but his smile

was a satisfied one as he vanished. It didn't take her long to realize that he must have held the Breakers' schedule before him when he'd arranged her trip. The team was scheduled to play L.A. on Thursday, Seattle on Friday, Portland on Sunday, and finally Golden State on Tuesday. She would catch the Lakers and Golden State—two out of four—not bad! And her scheduled flight home early Wednesday morning was—she would lay money on it—most likely the same one that would carry the team.

In the aftermath of Bill's magnanimous presentation Nia's mood did an abrupt about-face. The rest of Wednesday flew by in a whirl of excitement that touched nearly everyone with whom she came in contact. For the record, in a story she offered repeatedly through the day, she was looking forward both to the assignment and to a long-overdue visit with her family. Her heart's thrill, however, revolved around seeing Daniel.

By the time she was back in the house that night awaiting Daniel's call, however, she had grown apprehensive once more. It was a replay of that scene in Philadelphia, with a far deeper involvement now. Then he had been neither her loved one nor her lover. Now he was both. And with that deeper involvement, unfortunately, went much more to lose. Would he want her to come? Was he enjoying his freedom? Would he resent her intrusion, even though it had been managed by a well-intentioned third party? What could she expect to find?

This time, given the greater distance and the fact that, with no actual work in Los Angeles, she could always fly straight into San Francisco should Daniel not want her, she had decided not to take a chance on a surprise visit. As soon as he called she popped the news. His response was everything she might have hoped.

"You're kidding! Really? You'll be here tomorrow?"

"That's what the plane reservation says."

"That's great, Nia! How did you ever arrange it?"

"Actually, we have Bill Austen to thank. Dan . . . you don't mind . . . my, uh, intrusion?"

"Intrusion? Are you *crazy?* You couldn't have given me a nicer gift! God, it'll be good to see you!"

All her doubts erased, she gave him the number of her flight and her scheduled time of arrival. In the end they agreed that she should take a cab from the airport to the hotel, since the team's practice would overlap with her landing. Nia was just as happy at the prospect of waiting for him in his hotel room; the privacy would serve both their purposes.

It was therefore a total surprise to find him at the arrival gate waiting for her. She had left the plane in innocent appreciation of the warm sun, had crossed the tarmac with the rest of the passengers, expecting nothing more than to wait for her luggage—then had come to an abrupt stop when her eye caught that familiar face, standing out above the others in height, good looks, and a very poignant bridled excitement. Her heart picked up a rapid tattoo, and she moved with greater speed as Daniel separated himself from the crowd and came toward her. Instants later she was in his arms, being hugged tightly enough for the air to be crushed from her lungs, not caring in the least about the possibility of an audience when her feet actually left the pavement. He had a way of doing this to her—of sweeping away all traces of reality. When she was with him there was nothing in life that mattered more than he did.

He kissed her long and hard, there in the sunlight, in front of whoever cared to watch. When he finally drew back to look at her his expression held every bit of the pleasure she felt. "You look great, Nia," he gasped, then grinned. "New outfit?"

"You know it is, bub," she teased back, recalling that he had been with her when she had bought it—and the rest of her current possessions—the Saturday before. This was a particularly pretty ruffled skirt and blouse. With her height and long, slender legs, she wore it well. Additionally, she both looked and felt unusually feminine.

As though he followed her line of thought, he took her hand. "Let's get your bag. I could use a little more privacy for what I've got in mind."

What he had in mind was a direct trip back to the hotel and an equally straight bee-line to his room. When he had finally shut the door with its "Do Not Disturb" sign on the outer knob, he took her in his arms once more.

"Oh, I've missed you. . . ."

"It's only been three days," she whispered, loving him for his words and agreeing with them wholeheartedly.

"It seems more like three months!" His lips pressed sensuous kisses to her face and her neck.

"And you look so pretty. I'm almost going to hate taking this off." But his fingers moved to the front buttons of her blouse as she tugged at his tie, and before long they were naked in each other's arms, kissing and caressing with the hunger that three days' loneliness had built.

Daniel eased her back down to the sheets, covered her body with his, and entered her as smoothly as though their bodies had been one all along. Preliminaries were a luxury their mutual need did not allow. The leisurely savoring of flesh and curves, of muscles and hollows, would be for later. Now the race was toward fulfillment.

Nia loved Dan with every ounce of her being, rising to meet him, crying out as he filled her. In turn she held him to her greedily, adoring every inch of him. When the moment of inner explosion came it was a simultaneous experience of breathtaking beauty, a set of moments suspended in time—the pinnacle of love. As she lay against him in its aftermath her tears spread to the warmth of his chest to mingle with the sweat of their frenzied loving.

"Don't cry, babe. It's all right," he crooned, then caught his own uneven breath and held her more tightly.

She wondered. Would it be all right? Would she ever have Daniel Strahan as her own, truly her own? Would she ever have the glory of knowing that he would be hers tomorrow—and for every tomorrow that might exist? For that was how she wanted him—despite every rational argument against it. She did want him forever.

* * *

With the exception of the three hours spent at the Los Angeles Forum, Nia did not leave the hotel room once. For that matter, she didn't even dress—other than for the game and then the return trip to the airport on Friday morning. Daniel didn't do much better on that score, seeming to be perfectly at ease wandering around the room in the altogether, letting room service in with nothing but a towel knotted at his hip, feeling most happy in bed beside Nia.

The game itself was anti-climactic for them both, particularly since the playoff berth had already been secured. Daniel seemed totally immersed in her during the time they spent together, and though he gave the Breakers his intense concentration during court time, private time was totally private. Indeed, as he had said on that very first day she'd met him, his personal life *was* his own. At the time she had been sorry; now she could not have been more pleased.

The twenty-four hours went all too quickly. Long before she might have wished it, Nia was airborne for San Francisco, having left Daniel behind with the promise of a reunion three days hence, on Monday morning. Knowing she would see him then made leaving more bearable, as did the prospect of seeing her family.

It had been over four months since she'd been home. Both her parents were there to meet the plane, and their subsequent luncheon celebration was duly jubilant. She told them all about her work, including the project she had been sent west to do, a feature on silk screening in the San Franciscan art community. She told them about the fire in Cambridge and, at last, about Daniel. It had been her hope that he might join them all for dinner on Monday night at the house; her parents were totally agreeable. If they felt uneasy about Daniel's occupation and its coincidental relationship to their ex-son-in-law's, they said nothing. Their daughter was a grown woman, with a very distinct mind of her own. The fact that she was so obviously happy satisfied them.

Nia spent the rest of the day relaxing with her parents in Hillsborough. Their spacious family home was every bit as lovely as it had always seemed to her, even in those years of her rebellion. Now, as she wandered about, talking with her mother, then her father, then her brothers, when they sauntered in from college classes, she saw a beauty here she'd never quite recognized or been able to appreciate before. There was a warmth in this house, a sense of family. For the very first time she could identify with it.

As had been prearranged by Bill, Nia was busy enough on both Saturday and Sunday, interviewing artists and patrons of the arts, to keep her thoughts from her obsession with Daniel. Using her mother's car, she visited galleries and lofts, studios and workshops, where the cream of the local printmakers exhibited and worked. Though exhausted by Sunday night, she felt that she had gathered a wealth of information around which, with proper additional research, she could organize an interesting feature. She was even taken to dinner on Sunday evening by Bill Austen's counterpart on the *Western Edge* staff. And though the conversation was stimulating and the company easy, her sights were already set ahead to Monday morning and the plane that would be arriving at 10:35 from Oregon.

She was there to meet it half-an-hour early, took a seat by the arrival gate, and waited patiently for its approach. No one in the waiting room would have guessed that the attractive young woman in slim-fitting designer jeans and a dolman-sleeved vee-neck top of burgundy chenille, who sat with such a peaceful, almost beatific expression on her face was, in another life and a coast away, a spirited reporter. Nor would they have guessed that she was madly, passionately in love with Daniel Strahan, for she stood quietly while the passengers filed into the terminal in clumps of two and three, smiling brightly only when one separated himself from a group of giants and approached. They stood face to face for a minute, murmuring soft hellos until, in a simultaneous motion, each put an arm about the other's waist and they walked off down the busy corridor.

Their rendezvous in Los Angeles had been nearly complete in its privacy; their San Francisco sojourn was the opposite. Between the team meeting and practice that, of necessity, occupied Dan for most of Monday afternoon, and the dinner in Hillsborough that Nia's parents had given so graciously, they were barely able to exchange much more than the occasional soulful kiss. Nia had convinced him to spend the night at her parents' house; by the end of the evening she regretted the decision. For everything that a hotel room might have lacked in personal warmth, it would have afforded them the luxury of the privacy they craved. For Nia the intimacy of their lovemaking was the only means she had of expressing her love. In being denied that outlet she felt inordinately frustrated. It seemed the hardest thing she'd ever done to show him to his room later that night, then turn and retreat with her own quiet ache.

She barely made it to her own room. Damn it! Her parents knew that she was no longer a virgin! They also knew that she was nearly thirty! Her decision was made in a flash of rebellion reminiscent of days gone by. With a lighter heart she stripped, showered, and dressed in her robe and gown, then retraced her steps, barefooted, to the opposite end of the house. Without so much as a knock she entered the darkened room and shut the door behind her.

Daniel was in bed on his back, the sheets bunched carelessly across his hips, his chest bare and broad as his forearm covered his eyes. She assumed that he had just dozed off, for his breathing was slow and steady. He appeared to be totally oblivious to her entrance.

Pausing only to take off her robe and drop it over a chair, Nia crept forward and pulled the sheet back only far enough to slide in underneath and into bed beside him. His bodily warmth immediately reached out to her, and she nestled close against him. At that instant a strong arm came from nowhere to curve about her back and hold her even more snugly. Surprised but pleased, she looked up to meet Daniel's open amusement.

"I was wondering when you'd get here," he whispered with a roguish grin.

"You know me that well?" she whispered through her own sheepish smile.

"I know *us*. If you hadn't come here I would have gone looking for you."

Nia cuddled against him, resting her chin at the spot on his chest just above his nipple. His body hair was soft against her skin, his scent pure male. "That would have been cute! You don't know which room is mine."

"I'd have found it."

"You'd probably have found one of my brothers."

"They would have directed me."

"That sure of them, are you?"

"Uh-huh."

He had cause. Daniel Strahan had made a conquest of her family such as she would never have believed possible, particularly given her own past. By rights they should have been wary of him, perhaps somewhat in awe of his marginal star status, but wary nonetheless. Wariness was the last thing he had evoked tonight. And it was the last thing Nia felt right now. She had a totally different kind of conquest in mind and Daniel was in accord.

"Come here, babe," he whispered hoarsely as he pulled her over onto him, hauled her up his body so that her lips met his, and kissed her with every bit of the passion he'd felt all day but been unable to express. "I've missed you," he mumbled against her lips, then kissed her again and again.

Nia responded to him with the bounty of the love she felt. It was always this way between Daniel and her. Hadn't she known it would be? During the weeks they'd known each other before they'd become lovers they had both known that, once satisfied, the need would only increase. And so it had. Now, as the flow of passion raced hotly through her she could only run with it and see it to fulfillment. Her love would permit nothing less.

Daniel shifted and the bed creaked loudly. He froze, waited, then shook his head in dismay. He hadn't even noted the noise before; *then* there had been no cause! "Your mother is a wily woman," he moaned, then tested the springs again in a way that nearly drove Nia wild. With every move a telling groan arose from somewhere amid mattress, box spring, bed frame and hard oak floor. His sturdy weight would do it every time.

Nia smothered her disheartened laugh against his arm. "We could always sneak back to my bed. . . ."

"No way," he whispered more confidently. "This is a challenge. A test of our . . . our . . . compatibility."

"What do you mean—our compatibility? If we can't *do* anything—"

"Oh, we can do plenty. Just watch."

There was actually nothing to watch, for she soon closed her eyes and gave herself up to the wealth of sensation that Daniel proceeded to rouse in her. Every movement was slow and sensuous as, lying on their sides facing one another, he touched her body, tracing her curves through the silk of her nightgown, running his hand her slender length, then returning via the inside route to set her flesh aflame. She gasped when his hand moved higher, arching against him in mindless need, reaching to touch him as wonderingly, wanting to know that the simplicity of her touch could incite him as quickly.

The quiet of the night was broken only by their soft whispers and helpless gasps as each tried to control the urge to give in to frenzy. It was as much an exercise in self-control as in compatibility, and they passed with flying colors.

Nia thought there had never been anything as magnificent as the tall man stretched on his side before her. Her palm skimmed the sinewed swells of his chest and rounded his shoulder to run down his arm before dropping to his warm but rock-hard thigh. He wore a pair of briefs, more than he usually wore when they were together. Perhaps he hadn't been all that sure they'd be able to manage a nighttime tryst after all. She smiled. But she knew what would bring him pleasure and she pandered to it.

Daniel moaned softly at her ministrations, which had quickly, skillfully, made a mockery of his scant covering. "Oh, babe," he whispered raggedly, moments before he eased them completely off and reached for her. Still on their sides, he worked her gown up to her waist, cupped the softness of her bottom, and pulled her closer. One long, hair-roughened thigh slid between hers and she knowingly hooked her top leg higher.

"Nia . . ." he whispered again as he brought them together, then muffled her own outcry with his lips as he buried himself deep within her and held her tightly. "Don't move, babe. Just feel it," he rasped, his breath warm against her cheek. She could only purr her acknowledgment from the back of her throat, a feline sound of contentment. It would never have occurred to her to lie quietly like this, belying the internally ecstatic madness she felt. But then, she had taken so much in life for granted—until circumstances took a turn that reoriented things. Hadn't that been the case when she originally met Daniel? She had seen her life as perfectly satisfactory, until he had, unintentionally perhaps, shown her a world beyond.

Now he moved. Slowly. Carefully. With a sensual glide, an ebb and flow. The sensation was electric, a leisurely flame that grew hotter and hotter with each measured thrust until control became a poignant memory and she exploded into a world of unsuspected sensuality. As though her rapture triggered his own, Daniel tensed, then soared, clutching her against him with every bit of his strength.

The risk of discovery had been worth the glory of their passion, suffusing Nia with the glow that stayed with her for the rest of their stay. It was her mother, however, who put a name to it in those last moments at the airport on Wednesday morning.

"Do you love him, Antonia?" she whispered for Nia's ears alone as the two women stood, elbows linked, watching the stream of tall basketball players amble past. Daniel had already boarded; Nia would join him presently.

Her head swung to face her mother in surprise. But her mother most definitely knew. The question was only a formality. "Yes," she murmured softly. "Very much."

"He loves you."

"No." Nia looked down, frowned, shook her head slowly. "I don't know. He's got his life . . . his game. We get along well . . . beautifully. But I don't know if he actually *loves* me. He's vehement about the fact that he'll never tie a woman to his lifestyle. And he's certainly not ready to settle down."

"You're sure?" her mother asked with an undercurrent of doubt produced by her own observations. "He seemed very happy with us. Tom and Randy could barely get him to talk about basketball; they hadn't expected that he'd want to talk about much else, but his interest was in them, in us, in *you.*"

Nia wrinkled her nose in feigned nonchalance. "It'd never work, anyway. Even if he does love me, it'd never work."

"I don't know, Nia." Her mother smiled with a knowing air. "It seems to me it already does!"

Her mother had raised a point that, subconsciously or not, Nia had refused to consider. She had a lot to think about as she kissed her mother good-bye, hugged her father in turn, and then went on to join Daniel for the flight back to Boston.

ten

SOMETHING HAD CHANGED. IT WAS AN ALmost imperceptible altering of their relationship, a kind of subtle expectancy that hung in the air without resolution. Had it been purely an internal thing Nia might have attributed it to her mother's parting words and the thoughts they had triggered. But it came from Daniel as well, a sense of something being held back, of the final phrase not being said.

On the surface things were as lovely as before. Nia went to work on Thursday and Friday, arriving in Weston in time to watch the game each night, then had a late dinner waiting for Daniel when he returned. Their talk held a quiet poignancy, their lovemaking a strange urgency, as though each reached and reached for something he wasn't sure existed. In her heart Nia knew they were approaching a confrontation. But, guilty at her uncharacteristic timidity, she couldn't quite bring it about herself. If her confession of love would endanger that which they now had together, she would withhold it . . . at least a little longer.

It was, ironically, Harlan McKay who brought it all down to the wire. His phone calls had often interrupted their privacy; his less-than-enthusiastic grimace had met Nia's questioning gaze more than once. Trying to bear in mind Daniel's patient rationalization, she stoically ignored his very evident dislike of her. Until that Sunday afternoon . . . when she could no longer brush it aside.

The game had been the last of the regular season and a fairly easy win over San Antonio. Nia had made a point of being there, partly to be with Daniel, and partly to test her own strength. For with the Spurs came David Phillips; she hadn't seen him since meeting Daniel. As had been her greatest hope, she felt no pain at all when David saw her sitting close behind the Breaker bench and walked over to say hello. It was an entirely civil interchange on both sides and had proven something very important to Nia. It was this that she had hoped to tell Daniel as she waited in his office after the game. She had expected a longer delay than usual, what with the end-of-the-regular-season interviews and the obligatory locker room opening of champagne. The last person she had expected to appear in the office was Harlan McKay.

"Mr. McKay!" she exclaimed, standing quickly, not daring to call him by anything other than that formal title. Though Daniel never failed to use the more familiar Harlan, she was strangely intimidated by the man. And for good reason, it would appear.

"That's right, Mrs. Phillips." Had he put undue emphasis on the *Mrs.?* "I thought it was about time we had a talk."

Mustering her poise, Nia forced a smile. "You should be celebrating with your team. After all, they are the division champs."

"They're celebrating. I'm just going to make sure they *stay* the champs."

"Daniel agrees with you completely." She held her smile rigid as the back of her neck prickled in anticipation of a slowly falling bombshell. Harlan McKay was a large man, but there was nothing athletic about him. He had more the air of the domineering patriarch—which gave her a clue as to his purpose in seeking her out, moments before he thrust aside all pleasantry to make his point.

"I know what Daniel says, Mrs. Phillips. I've known Daniel for a lot longer than you have." She had no argument with that. All she could do was wait for him to continue, which he did quite summarily. "I want you to stay away from him," he ordered in a coarsely demanding tone.

"What?" She hadn't expected outright hostility.

"I believe you heard me."

"I think I did," she shot back, feeling an instinctive sense of anger. "I just don't think I understand."

"That's too bad," he commented coolly. "I thought you were a little more intelligent than average. Let me spell it out for you."

She frowned. "I wish you would."

Harlan leveled his gaze and shot her a look of pure venom. "I don't want you to have anything more to do with Daniel Strahan. The season's over; you can pack your bags and get out. He doesn't need you . . . or anyone outside this organization."

"I can't believe you're saying this—"

"Well, believe it!" he thundered, then quieted. "You've disrupted his life enough as it is. We have the playoffs coming and I want him to be in top shape. With you hanging on to him he can't possibly be."

"Does Daniel know you're talking with me?" she asked in sudden defiance. If Daniel Strahan fought to win, so did she. And she was not about to fold before any autocrat, self-proclaimed or otherwise!

"I know what's best for Dan," he answered without answering.

"He may disagree."

"Well, *I* know what's best for *my team,* and that includes Daniel. I've seen him with you day after day, rushing out of here to go to you, sitting with you in airplanes and restaurants. I know that you're living with him. And I'm sure that you're the reason why he arrived in San Diego late. Something personal—hell! The team is the only thing that should be occupying his mind, not some divorcée." His lip curled in disgust as she paled.

"What does my past have to do with this?"

Harlan shook his head at his cleverness and smiled. "I saw you talking with David Phillips today. I had heard those stories about a little wife tucked away, too. It wasn't until I saw the two of you together that I realized you must have been the one."

"What does that have to do with anything?" she cried, feeling herself being backed into a corner.

"You're a hanger-on. You must have some fixation with the game of basketball. You would never have been interested in Daniel had he not been involved—"

"That's a lie! You have no idea what you're saying!" Nia felt her insides beginning to tremble and tipped her chin higher.

Harlan's voice suddenly lowered to a dangerously soft note. "Oh, I know precisely what I'm saying. And that is that if you help me, I'm prepared to help you."

Totally uncomprehending, she frowned in disbelief. "You're crazy."

"Is Jimmy Mahoney crazy, Mrs. Phillips?" That was the bombshell she had been subconsciously awaiting. Its force knocked the wind from her lungs and it took her a minute to find her voice again.

"Jimmy Mahoney?"

His eyes opened wider in pleasure at her anxiety. "The mayor of Boston . . . ?"

"I know who Jimmy Mahoney is, Mr. McKay. Please tell me where he fits into this scenario."

"I understand that you've had some trouble with him."

She stiffened. "That's on the record."

"So it is," he drawled. "An outstanding libel suit for shoddy reporting—not a very good reference."

"Now that's a slight distortion of the facts." She stood up to him indignantly.

"Whatever." He shrugged as though it didn't

matter in the least. "You're still in trouble. It could mean an ugly lawsuit and when you lose—"

"*If* I lose."

"You will. Mahoney has power. And you will find yourself out of a job and without hope of finding another."

Nia lowered her head, put her fingertips to her forehead, and studied the floor. Though the relevance of this all to the present situation was still lost on her, she felt a rising sense of anger and made no effort to stem it. When she looked up, her eyes held dark, violet rage.

"I smell blackmail, Mr. McKay, but I don't understand the details. Exactly what are you getting at?"

"Hmmmm, maybe you're bright after all." His smile was deceptive and faded on command. "We'll see . . . if you accept my offer."

"And what *is* your offer?" she demanded.

"I said it before. You help me. I help you."

Nia put a hand on her hip. "Elaborate. I guess I'm not all that bright after all. I want to hear you explain it so that I understand completely."

Harlan's gaze narrowed. "You help me by disappearing from Daniel's life. I help you by swinging my weight with Mahoney."

"So that's it," she whispered as comprehension finally dawned. "You know Jimmy Mahoney."

"Very well."

"And you'd actually go to bat on my behalf if I cooperate with you?"

"Or against you . . . if you refuse."

Nia threw up her hands in exasperation and paced to the far side of the room before turning.

"And you *really* think that my simply . . . disappearing . . . would be the best thing for Daniel?"

"I know it would. You've been taking up too much of his time. He used to put basketball first. He used to be there whenever I needed him. He used to answer my calls at any hour. Now he rushes me off the phone . . . to be with you!"

As Nia stared at Harlan in disbelief at his tirade she recalled Daniel's words. Harlan *did* appear to be jealous. He sounded almost hurt that Daniel had chosen her over him. But did he have the power to swing that libel suit one way or the other, particularly since she trusted Bill's feeling that any danger of an actual suit was past? This was no pouting child who confronted her. This was a grown man who wielded more than his share of power. And though there was no way she wanted that power directed against her, she could no more grant his wish than she could deny her love for Daniel.

"I'm sorry, Mr. McKay." She spoke softly but firmly, tautly controlling her anger. "I can't help you."

"Can't? What kind of a fool are you? You'd throw away your life, your career, to chase an . . . an elusive dream?"

Nia's voice held the force of conviction. "When the dream is of love, I'd chase it anywhere."

"Hmmph!" he sneered. "What kind of an answer is *that?* It's purely feminine and totally absurd!"

"That's where you're wrong, Harlan," a deep voice cut in sharply. Both heads whipped toward it.

Nia was the first to recover. "Daniel!" she whispered, eyes wide, unsure of what he'd heard, what he'd thought. He was very obviously furious. Had she been wrong to speak up to Harlan? Had she presumed too much?

Daniel straightened from the doorjamb and walked toward her. In those moments she felt that her future was at center court, up for grabs. His body was tall and taut, his eyes dark brown, nearly black in the throes of emotion.

"Daniel?" she whispered again, pleading the case for her love in the cry of his name.

"It's all right, babe," he murmured, smiling wanly as he put an arm around her, then turned to face Harlan, who seemed suddenly nervous.

"How long were you standing there?" the older man asked.

"Long enough to hear your threat."

Harlan put out a hand in a pacifying gesture. "Now, listen, Dan—"

"No, Harlan, you listen to me!" Daniel exploded with an anger that sent shudders through Nia. Had his arm not been around her, holding her close, she might have shied away herself. "You listen to me, because I'm only going to say this once. If you ever, *ever* make a threat like that again I'll personally take *you* to court. It so happens that I love this woman and if she'll have me I intend to marry her." Nia's heart soared skyward, but Daniel wasn't done. "I've given the Breakers more than fourteen years of my life and in that time I have never given you cause for disappointment. If you think that my relationship with Antonia is affecting my ability to coach, you can fire me. It's as simple as that!" He softened as he looked sideways. "Let's go, Nia. We've got a lot to talk about."

Harlan McKay was left standing with his jaw hanging, but Nia had already pushed him from her mind. Daniel was beside her, leading her through the last of the lingering Breaker fans, out of the arena and into the late afternoon sunshine. He said nothing, simply held her hand with a fierce possessiveness, releasing it only after he had tucked her into the Datsun.

"Daniel . . . ?" she began when he slid behind the wheel, but he held out a hand to silence her.

"Let's go home first, babe. Give me a minute to cool off."

She would give him as much time as he needed, providing he repeated to her what he had told Harlan in anger short moments before. Had it been an idle threat? Had he simply spoken out in anger? Had he exaggerated his feelings to make his point with Harlan?

The drive to his house took an eternity as Nia's heart and future hung in the balance. When they finally arrived Daniel took her hand again and led her away from the house, out toward the woods in back. He said nothing until they had wandered far enough for the trees to obliterate any intruding signs of humanity. Then he dropped her hand, buried his own in the pockets of his slacks, and turned to face her. His eyes were rich with a feeling that didn't quite spill to his face, which held a look of deep, dark tension. Nia was convinced, in that instant, that he was going to confess that he'd lied to Harlan after all. When he didn't speak, she could stand the suspense no longer.

"Well?" she asked falteringly. *"Do* you love me . . . or," she looked around at the encompassing solitude and grinned cynically, "are you going to murder me, chop me in little pieces, and bury them with no witnesses?"

The first of the tension flowed helplessly from him as he smiled. "You think you're pretty smart, don't you?"

"Actually . . . no. I've been pretty dumb about all this."

"About what?"

"About not telling you how I feel."

Not sure just how to take her words, Daniel simply continued to stare at her. She thought she saw fear and regret and longing, but she was so emotionally involved that it was hard to decipher fact from fancy. She wanted him to love her so badly.

"I love you, Daniel." It was a confession long overdue. His eyes widened and brightened; his features seemed to relax. But still he didn't speak. "Do *you* love *me?"*

Very, very slowly, the manly lips she adored curved into a smile. And he nodded. "You heard me say it."

"Did you mean it? Or was it said in the heat of anger?"

"It was said in the heat of anger, but I meant every word."

"About wanting to marry me, too?"

"That, too."

"Oh, Dan . . ." was all she had time to say before he had wiped out the distance between them once and for all, and swept her into his embrace as though she were the greatest prize of all.

His kiss was deep and loving, just as it had been for so very long without her daring to accept it as such. "I do love you, Nia, and I do want you to marry me."

She couldn't have heard more beautiful words, yet she had to know now, to ask everything. "You once said you would never ask a woman to share your kind of existence. Have you really changed your mind?"

"Uh-huh." His confident smile left no doubt.

"Why? What made you change it?"

The thinking had all been done in those lonely hours away from her, or in the middle of the night when he'd awoken and lain beside her, fearing that one day she'd be gone. He knew his mind now, and was ready to speak it. "You made the change, Nia. From the first I knew you were special. More than special. You were everything I wanted in a woman. Every attempt to keep you at arm's length failed. Even though I knew how badly you'd been hurt once, I just couldn't picture *my* life without you. Then, because of you and what I wanted to do with you, I discovered that basketball *was* only a job. I was very happy to leave it after a game, having found something that meant so much more to me."

"But what about your doctorate?"

"That was—is—more a profession than a passion. Yes, it means a lot to me, but it, too, has its place. I always knew that it would have to wait until my basketball days were over."

"But they're not—"

"Not yet. I doubt that Harlan will can me at this stage. But I do think I'd like to retire within another year or two."

"To be a psychologist?"

"That. And . . . to be a husband, or *more* than a husband, perhaps even a father."

Nia caught her breath. "You really think it would work?"

"It *has* worked! That's the point!" Hadn't her mother said as much? Hadn't she herself come to agree? But to hear it from Daniel—that was something else! He spoke on, and she listened in silent ecstasy. "When I wanted to be here with you after the fire I decided to join the team a day late. It would never have occurred to me to do that before, but, you know," he grinned in self-mockery, "they survived without me. Then, when I needed you so badly during that road trip, there you were. I know that things may not always be as convenient; there may be times when we *have* to be apart. But I want to help you settle the house, to be by your side if Mahoney opens his mouth again. I want to take you on the road with me whenever you can work it around your assignments. You're as stubborn as I am; if we decide to make it work, it will!" He paused, took a breath. "That's what changed my mind. For the first time I found someone who mattered enough to make it worthwhile to try!"

"Oh, Daniel, I love you," she murmured, knowing then that everything would be all right, that her future was secure. Her cheek pressed against his shirt, she coiled her arms tightly around his waist. "I love you."

"But will you marry me?" he drawled, half in earnest.

"Did you have any doubt that I would?" she returned, drawing back to gaze up at his handsome face.

"You *did* have a bad experience once before," he confronted her softly. "It's possible that you wouldn't want to try."

"If I don't try," her violet eyes flooded, "I condemn myself to a life of emptiness. You make everything so much richer." She raised a finger to blot her lower lashes. "And besides," she sniffled, then grinned, "now you've appealed to my streak of determination. We'll make it work. I know we will!"

"That's it, babe," he crooned, hugging her soundly. "That's the spunky woman I love! I don't care if she tells me where to get off every once in a while as long as she tells me she loves me here and there along the way."

Nia tipped her head back with a blinding smile. "You, Mr. Strahan, have got yourself a deal!"

It was much, much later that night, after they'd sated the needs of the flesh to their mutual, albeit temporary, satisfaction, that they spoke of the immediate future. "The team will be back and forth to

Washington for the first-round playoffs, Nia. Can we be married by Wednesday, before the series begins?"

"I don't see why not," she answered, drunk enough on his love to agree to almost anything he said.

"Will you come down for the games there?"

"I don't see why not." She sighed her contentment and stretched against his naked length.

"You can do the researching for your article then?"

"I don't see why not."

He pinched her middle playfully. "Is there anything you'd object to right now?"

"You bet!" she snapped. "I'd violently object if you left this bed to do anything but—"

"What about the TV? Would you mind if I watched a rerun of the game?"

Nia regarded him indulgently, knowing she'd be unable to deny him anything he truly wanted. "You *really* want to watch a rerun of the game?"

"I might," he tested her.

"OK." She grinned. "You can turn it on . . . on one condition."

"Uh-oh." He rolled his eyes. "One condition. What is it?"

"You've got to watch in here."

"In the bedroom?"

"That *is* where we are."

He shammed dismay. "But the recorder is in the other room." It was. And the last thing that would suit her purposes would be for him to risk a hernia carting the large set around.

"Then . . . let's go in there . . . like this."

"We're not dressed!"

"Since when does that bother you?" Her eyes sparkled with humor.

Daniel was adorable in his feigned innocence. "Nia, I'm the *coach.* Coaches don't go to games *nude!*"

A ripple of laughter shot through her before she could contain it. "That's terrific! Then, let's take this blanket. Stand up."

He stood obediently as she hauled the blanket from the bed, tossed one end up over his shoulders, and draped them together with the makeshift shawl.

"There!" she exclaimed. "Will this do?"

His hand slid over the softness of her beneath the blanket. "It'll do."

"Let's go, then. The game is about to start."

They managed to reach the living room with a minimum of bumps and contortions, and those, she was sure, were contrived by the coach. But if he wanted to watch the game, the game it would be. Daniel held her beside him as he headed for the set, pressed the proper buttons, then turned her around and collapsed on the sofa, dropping the remote control switch on the table nearby.

"There," he panted in exaggerated exhaustion. "Sit here . . . no, this way . . . a little to the left . . ."

Nia twisted and squirmed against him, following his directions even as she wondered whether he knew what he was doing. But he *had* to know; that was no ghost of passion she felt in him.

"There I am," he grinned, pointing to the set as

the pregame show commenced. Nia followed the direction of his finger and failed to notice that it instantly disappeared beneath the blanket. "Hmmm, I look like I've gained weight."

"You *always* look heavier on television," she chided, feeling his warm touch inching its erotic way around her body.

"I don't know," he bent his head to nibble at the tip of her ear, "maybe I should grow a beard."

"Don't you dare," she gasped as that stealthy hand slid sensuously over the firming swell of her breast, moving slowly back and forth with maddeningly precise effect.

"Why not?" he asked innocently as he lowered his other hand to her thigh.

"Because . . . your very slight five o'clock shadow . . . is sexy." He was sexy right now and she wasn't even looking at him. But her body tingled at his touch and she inched further back against him. "There you go." She eyed the set, from which he suddenly disappeared. "That was quick!" The camera moved back, then closed in on the sportscaster.

"It always is," he murmured between soft samplings of her neck. "These professional athletes aren't all that bright, you know. Don't expect any coach to sustain an intelligent conversation for very long. Two minutes is about his limit."

"Two minutes?" She squirmed as the fingers of his lower hand crept to the inside of her thigh. "Is that all?"

"Um-hmmm."

Now there were two sportcasters in colorful

conversation, their headphones and mouthpieces solidly in place to ensure that the roar of the crowd was no more than a background accompaniment to the commentary in progress.

"Are you listening, Dan?" she moaned, slowly losing track of reality. She certainly couldn't hear what the television said—the roar of blood through her veins was far too loud for that.

"Listening?" he asked blankly.

"The show . . . you wanted to watch." She looked up over her shoulder at him, then slowly swiveled in his arms. Behind her, the crowd grew quiet.

"Hmmm . . . so I did." He smiled, but he only watched Nia now.

"I love you," she whispered, aglow from within. "I always will." Their eyes were locked together in visual mating, in total understanding.

Deafened to all but their syncopated hearts, they barely heard the soulful opening strains of the national anthem, slow and full-bodied as it wafted into the air. His hand trembling, Daniel traced the softness of her features one by one. The gentleness of his touch matched the adoration in his eyes, and Nia exulted in them both. When his thumb brushed her lips they parted eagerly, to be rewarded moments later by the richness of his kiss. It was a kiss filled with promise, a kiss filled with love. Above all, it was a new beginning.

Blinded by passion, and lost in their love, Daniel groped for the remote control and switched the television off.